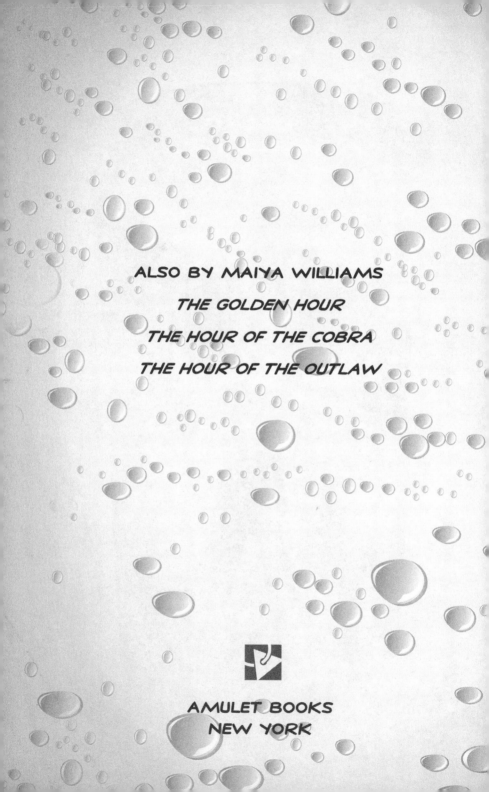

ALSO BY MAIYA WILLIAMS

THE GOLDEN HOUR

THE HOUR OF THE COBRA

THE HOUR OF THE OUTLAW

AMULET BOOKS
NEW YORK

LIBRARY OF CONGRESS CATALOGING-IN-PUBLICATION DATA
WILLIAMS, MAIYA.
THE FIZZY WHIZ KID / BY MAIYA WILLIAMS.
P. CM.
SUMMARY: MOVING TO HOLLYWOOD WITH HIS ACADEMIC PARENTS, ELEVEN-YEAR-OLD MITCH FEELS LIKE AN OUTSIDER IN HIS SCHOOL, WHERE EVERYONE HAS CONNECTIONS TO THE POWERFUL AND FAMOUS IN THE ENTERTAINMENT INDUSTRY, UNTIL HE IS CAST IN A SODA COMMERCIAL THAT LAUNCHES A POPULAR CATCHPHRASE.
ISBN 978-0-8109-8347-2
[1. FAME FICTION. 2. MOVING, HOUSEHOLD FICTION. 3. HOLLYWOOD (LOS ANGELES, CALIF.) FICTION.] I. TITLE.
PZ7.W66687FI 2010
[FIC] DC22

TEXT COPYRIGHT © 2010 MAIYA WILLIAMS
ILLUSTRATIONS COPYRIGHT © 2010 MICHAEL KOELSCH
BOOK DESIGN BY CHAD W. BECKERMAN

PRINTED AND BOUND IN U.S.A.
10 9 8 7 6 5 4 3 2 1

AMULET BOOKS ARE AVAILABLE AT SPECIAL DISCOUNTS WHEN PURCHASED IN QUANTITY FOR PREMIUMS AND PROMOTIONS AS WELL AS FUNDRAISING OR EDUCATIONAL USE. SPECIAL EDITIONS CAN ALSO BE CREATED TO SPECIFICATION. FOR DETAILS, CONTACT SPECIALMARKETS@ABRAMSBOOKS.COM OR THE ADDRESS BELOW.

ABRAMS
THE ART OF BOOKS SINCE 1949
115 WEST 18TH STREET
NEW YORK, NY 10011
WWW.ABRAMSBOOKS.COM

FOR ROBIN
AND BLAKE
WITH LOVE

CONT

ENTS

1

The New Kid

SOME PEOPLE RACE DIRT BIKES. SOME people collect snow globes. Some people build boats in a bottle. My mom's hobby is baking desserts. Man, do I love her hobby— it's so much better than boats in a bottle! My dad's hobby also happens to be his job. He's an entomologist, which is a scientist who studies bugs. I don't like his hobby as much; it's kind of weird. Actually, I have a pretty weird hobby myself. I make lists.

WHY I LIKE LISTS

1. Useful for organizing thoughts
2. Fast way to give information to others
3. Easier to read than paragraphs

I've been making lists since first grade, when I first learned how to write. Nobody knows why; it's a family mystery.

OTHER FAMILY MYSTERIES

1. Why does my mom always get the hiccups when she laughs?

2. Why is my dad the only person on the planet who loves cockroaches?

3. What is that weird smell coming from the back of the refrigerator?

4. Why do people in uniforms make my mom nervous?

5. Why does my mom care so much about manners?

6. Why do we keep moving?

The family-mystery list could go on for pages. But instead of that, here's a list about me.

FACTS ABOUT MITCHELL MATHIS

- Age twelve, sixth grade
- Average height, weight
- Pretty good student, but no Einstein
- Pets: black Labrador retriever—"Bandit"
- Favorite book: "The Jungle Book," by Rudyard Kipling
- Favorite food: fried chicken, Mom's chocolate cake
- Favorite sports: baseball, football, ice hockey
- Favorite car: yellow Lamborghini

- Favorite animal: big cats (jaguars, tigers, lions, cheetahs, etc.)
- Favorite activities: making lists, handball, skateboarding, juggling, magic, playing with Bandit, playing guitar, going to the opera (no lie!), exploring, and discovering stuff
- Biggest fear: looking like an idiot
- Best personal trait: I've got guts

FIVE THINGS THAT TAKE GUTS

1. Skateboarding on the highway
2. Staring down a pit bull with a pork chop tied to your neck
3. Standing in front of a 100 mph fastball, with no helmet
4. Eating fifty hot chili peppers with no bread or water
5. Starting a new school after fall session has already begun

Okay, I haven't done the first four things. But I've done the fifth thing on the list many times, and when this whole mess started I was going to do it again. Frankly, I'd prefer to eat the fifty chili peppers.

You may not think it's very hard to start a new school after it's already begun, but you would be very, very wrong. This has been my experience: Weeks before I even get there, somebody's know-it-all mom hears that a new kid (me) is moving into the neighborhood and will be attending the school. She tells her kid. Her kid takes this news to the classroom, and the rumors about the new kid (me) start flying: I'm a genius, I'm a dummy, I'm rich, I'm poor, I was kicked out of my last school, I'm in the witness protection program, I have an identical twin brother growing out of my left shoulder. (None of these things is true. See "Facts About Mitchell Mathis" list.)

Then the big day arrives. I check in at the office. The principal walks me down the hall, like a prisoner on his way to his execution. The principal opens a door, interrupting the class, and introduces me. He gets my name wrong, so I politely correct him. After he leaves, the teacher finds a seat for me, usually one within spitball distance of the meanest kid in the class. Then she assigns somebody to be my "buddy," usually the class egghead. For the rest of the day, I'm stuck walking around the school with the guy nobody else would be caught dead with, who tells me a lot of boring details about the school but leaves out the real important stuff.

STUFF YOU REALLY WANT TO KNOW ABOUT A SCHOOL

1. Which bathroom is the good one (safest, least gross, etc.)
2. Which cafeteria food is nasty and which is okay
3. Which water fountains will spray you in the face, and which ones just give a dribble
4. Which yard monitors are the crabbiest
5. Which bullies deliver expert wedgies

This last point is important. I've gotten a lot of wedgies in my day, and they are not pleasant. But I've learned from my mistakes. The main thing I've learned is that first impressions are everything.

TEN THINGS NOT TO DO ON THE FIRST DAY OF SCHOOL (BECAUSE THEY MAKE YOU LOOK LIKE A JERK)

1. Don't get a haircut the day before.
2. Don't wear brand-new white sneakers.
3. DON'T HAVE YOUR MOM WITH YOU. (Seriously, don't.)
4. Don't wear pants that are too short.
5. Don't wear hats, jewelry, or cowboy boots.

6. Don't carry a lunch box with a picture of a TV show on it.

7. Don't reveal that you like opera music.

8. If you're really good at something, like, for instance, juggling, don't juggle until at least a month goes by, or people will think you're a show-off.

9. Don't hang around with the class egghead.

AND MOST IMPORTANT:

10. DON'T STAND OUT.

But here's the thing about lists—no matter how much you try to use them to prepare yourself, sometimes they let you down. Sometimes they're not complete, and you don't know it until it's too late. I went over that list a hundred times, but nothing could prepare me for DeMille Elementary. I didn't know it then, but I was already doomed.

My family had just moved to Hollywood, California, and we hadn't fully settled in yet. Our house was filled with packing boxes, and I didn't know where anything was, so we had to buy a backpack, even though I already had one that I really liked packed in a box somewhere. Of course the stores didn't have very many backpacks left, but I managed to get one that didn't look too stupid.

Remember: First impressions are everything.

My mom dropped me off at the principal's office, where I met Principal Lang. He led me out of the main building and past a bunch of long, rectangular buildings called "bungalows." Each one held two classrooms. He opened the door to bungalow twelve, and all eyes shifted to the source of the disruption: me. I can read people pretty well. You could even say I'm gifted in that area. Those eyes were all saying the same thing: *I'm glad I'm not you, you poor jerk.*

"Excuse me, Mrs. Samuelson," Principal Lang said. "I'd like to introduce your new student. This is Matthew Mitchell. He'll be joining your class. . . ."

"It's Mitchell Mathis. . . ." I said.

"What?"

"My last name is Mathis," I repeated a little louder. "Mitch Mathis."

"I'm sorry. Anyway, Mitchell comes to us from St. Paul, Minnesota. I'm sure everyone here will make him feel welcome." Principal Lang paused to admire the autumn wall decorations and then clapped his hands together. "Well! I'll leave you to it!" He couldn't get out of the classroom fast enough.

Mrs. Samuelson was middle-aged, with short, gray-brown hair, glasses, and a stocky build, and something about her made me like her right away . . . maybe it was the fact that she kind of smelled like pancakes.

"Mitchell, why don't you take that empty seat?" Mrs. Samuelson pointed to the front desk in the third row, the one right in front of a kid with jet-black hair that fell over one of his eyes, making him look like a punk pirate. He wore a black T-shirt with a skull on it, black jeans, and green sneakers, and he had a diamond stud in his nose. He was fidgeting with a ballpoint pen, clicking it in and out, in and out, in and out, *click click click*. . . . Already I wanted a new seat.

"You came at a very good time," Mrs. Samuelson continued. "We're right in the middle of social studies, and this week we are doing a lesson on heritage and family history. Today we are talking about our names. You see, your name says a lot about you, your parents, and their values. Everyone was given the assignment to find out where his or her name came from." She looked out at the class. "Who would like to start?"

A flurry of hands shot up.

"Okay, okay," Mrs. Samuelson said, and laughed. "Dash, why don't you go first. Stand, state your full name, and tell us where it came from."

A tall boy with dark, curly hair and glasses stood up. He

was rail thin and had an elegant but slightly bored attitude, like a British aristocrat.

"Dashiell Bogart Silverman. Dash for short. I was named after my parents' favorite mystery writer, Dashiell Hammett, and their favorite film noir actor, Humphrey Bogart. 'Film noir' is what they call those black-and-white crime movies of the nineteen forties, and a lot of these movies were based on Dashiell Hammett's stories. See, film noir, crime, and mystery are my parents' hobby. They're both film writers, and they met in college at a screening of *The Maltese Falcon*, which, by the way, starred Humphrey Bogart and was based on a novel by Dashiell Hammett. We have the DVD of *The Maltese Falcon*, so I've probably seen it a hundred times. It's very cool."

Dash sat down with a satisfied smile on his face. You could tell he loved where his name came from. Next, a girl stood up, her crazy-looking red hair held back by a headband decorated with fake bumblebees. She pushed her glasses up on her nose, and her voice clicked along like a typewriter.

"Julia Jodie Schwartz. My dad is a talent agent at Creative Quest Agency, and I was named after his two highest-earning female clients. Interesting fact: If I had been born a boy, my name would've been Brad Tom Johnny Schwartz, based on my dad's highest-earning male clients. Unfortunately, last year these two female clients were stolen from my dad by a competing talent agency, which was totally disloyal of them. My dad spent a lot of time building their careers! If it weren't for him, they'd be waiting tables at Jerry's Deli! Anyway, we don't talk about them anymore. My dad refuses to even say their names, so now my parents just call me J.J."

J.J. sat down. There was a pause as everyone waited for the next person to speak, a really pretty girl with short blond hair, cut like a boy's, and big blue eyes. She was staring out the window, but not at anything in particular. J.J. turned around and pounded the girl's desk. She turned, surprised.

"Is it my turn?" She stood up. She wore an outfit that looked like she'd dug it out of the thrift-shop grab bag: the kind of vest my grandpa would wear over a T-shirt, dress, rainbow-striped leggings, and knee-high moccasin boots. On anyone else it would have looked crazy, but it looked okay on her. "I'm Tangerine Dream Bestor. Both of my parents are actors. They're very creative, so they didn't want to give me an ordinary name. They wanted to give me a name that was meaningful and important, so they named me after their favorite fruit."

She sat down and looked back out the window to the muffled snickers of the class.

"Tangie, perhaps you can tell us where the 'Dream' part of your name came from," Mrs. Samuelson prompted, trying to hide her own amusement. Tangie blinked and rose to her feet again. She was so mellow, it seemed as if everything she did was in slow motion.

"Well, a tangerine is a healthy food that feeds your body, but dreams are food for the soul. Without our dreams we are nothing. They're what drive us and keep us going in hard times. You have to have both to be a complete person, right? It's all about balance."

Wow, that answer wasn't bad! She drifted back to her seat as gently as a leaf settling. I could tell that at least some kids in the class had a new respect for her. Now I wished my name was like hers, maybe something like . . . Pineapple Courage Mathis.

But when it was my turn I stood up and said, "My name is Mitchell Christopher Mathis, and I was named after my two grandfathers—my dad's father's name is Mitchell, and my mom's father's name is Christopher. I prefer Mitch." Then I sat down. Pretty boring, I thought. So did everybody else.

The punk pirate behind me stood up. Actually, it was more like he *jumped* up. He moved fast, like a squirrel. Like a squirrel who'd drunk too much coffee.

"I'm Skywalker Ortega, as you all know," he said quickly. "No middle name, so I'm forced to use the wacky first name. If it's not obvious, my dad's favorite movie of all time is *Star Wars*, and his favorite character is Luke Skywalker. Why he didn't name me Luke, I don't know—I guess it's kind of a joke, but it's no worse than being named after a citrus fruit."

"It could be worse. You could've been named Jar Jar Binks," Dash called out. Everyone laughed.

As kids continued down the rows, I started to see a pattern developing. Out of twenty-eight kids, ten were named after actors. Seven were named after movie characters. Five were named after book characters or authors. Three were named after something in nature, and only three had family names, like me. It was the first clue that I was doomed . . . but I'll get to that soon enough.

After everyone had a chance to talk about his or her name, we had a math lesson, then we went to the music room, and then it was time for lunch. Mrs. Samuelson had asked Dash to show me around. Dash had a weird habit of leaning forward while he walked, like his head wanted to get someplace and couldn't wait for the rest of his body to catch up.

"DeMille Elementary has what you call an 'open plan,'" he said. "It's really a bunch of bungalows surrounding a courtyard. Kindergarten through third-grade classrooms have their own playground, and fourth through sixth grade get the upper yard. Here's the library," he said, leading me up to a cluster of bungalows. "You've already seen the music room, and the next door is the computer room." He pointed at a door. "Don't go in this bathroom unless you enjoy walking through toilet water. There's always a clogged one in there."

We walked farther, past a building with the words LANGLEY GYMNASIUM painted in huge letters on the outside.

"Who's Langley?" I asked.

"I don't know, some dead guy. Now, over here we have the lunch tables and the cafeteria," he said, pointing to the line of windows. "Don't order the broccoli cheese pasta. Ever. And on Fridays watch out for airborne pudding cups."

I liked this guy.

Since we had both brought our lunches that day, we didn't stop at the cafeteria, but just sat at one of the tables on the patio outside. A group of kids from the class joined us—Skywalker, Tangie, J.J., and Brandon, a blond kid with neatly trimmed hair, a lime-green polo shirt, and creased slacks. Brandon Samuel Goldwyn was named after his great-great-grandfather, who started a movie studio called Metro-Goldwyn-Mayer, or MGM, in the nineteen twenties. He seemed to think that made him king of the classroom. I could tell Dash didn't care much for Brandon; he bristled as Brandon brushed crumbs off the table before sitting.

"We're taking a poll," J.J. said. "What's the funniest show on TV? Not classic TV. The show has to be in production right now."

"*Monty Montgomery's House of Weird* is the best thing on TV," Dash said. "His sketches are brilliant."

"Brilliant?" Brandon scoffed. "They barely make any sense."

"Yeah, well, it's for people who have read a few books—you know, people who think." You know how you get an uncomfortable feeling, like you don't want to be somewhere but you can't leave? That's what I was feeling. But Brandon didn't seem to mind Dash's jab.

"Hey, like my dad always says, 'If it's a thinker, it's a stinker,'" Brandon said with a shrug. "As far as I'm concerned, the *House of Weird* is the House of Boring."

"Oh yeah? Well, what do you watch?" Dash snorted. "Let me guess, something with a lot of poop jokes."

"*Down and Dirty*."

"You've got to be kidding!" Dash howled. "That idiotic show is like the amateur hour! It's embarrassing that it's even on the air!"

"Yeah," Skywalker agreed, tossing his hair out of his eyes with a flick of his head. It fell right back. "The production values are really cheap."

"It's the top-rated show on Friday primetime," Brandon pointed out. "And it's got an eighteen share. You guys may not like it, but the rest of America does."

"What about *Kiss the Bride*?" Tangie said, to break up the argument. "It's really big in England. . . ."

"I prefer the American version, *Kick the Bride*," J.J. said. "It's just more accessible. What do you think, Mitch?"

They all turned to me. I was completely lost. Production values? Primetime? Eighteen share? It's like they were speaking another language.

"Yes, Mitch," said Tangie. "What do you think is the funniest show on TV?"

"You know, I really don't watch a lot of television," I admitted.

"What's the matter—TV's not good enough for you?" J.J. said. "I'm sick of you movie snobs. Listen, TV has some really great stuff. You're missing out—"

"I don't watch movies either," I interrupted. "My family never really got into that."

Now everyone looked confused.

"You're kidding. How about *Star Wars*? You have to have seen *Star Wars* episodes one, two, three, four, five, or six, right?" Skywalker asked.

"Well, I've heard of them of course, and I know the story, sort of, but no, I haven't actually seen any of them. I've flipped through some of the books. . . ."

"The *Star Wars* saga is not a book!" Skywalker laughed.

"Wow, you're really serious! Wow." He shook his head, unable to say more.

"Hey, a lot of people don't go to the movies," Tangie said, coming to my defense. "Renting is a lot cheaper, and you can watch it in your own house."

"I think he's saying he doesn't watch any TV or movies in any form at all," Brandon said, one eyebrow raised. "Isn't that right, Mitch? Not even on an airplane, right?"

"That's impossible," J.J. said. "I mean, unless you belong to some kind of weird cult or something. . . ." She turned to me with a suspicious look.

There was an eerie silence. Then I felt Dash tugging my arm. "Come on, Mitch, I want to show you the gym."

"But we already saw the . . ."

Dash dragged me away before I could finish. After we got a fair distance from the others, he turned to me.

"You were joking, right? About not watching any TV or movies?"

"Well, you can't watch a lot of TV when you don't own a TV. . . ."

Dash put his hands on his hips and looked up to the sky, like I had presented him with some big problem. "Mitch. Let me give you a little history lesson. Right now we are standing in DeMille Elementary, right? That's *Cecil B. DeMille* Elementary. Cecil B. DeMille was a major movie director. He produced and directed a whole bunch of films—won tons of awards—but one thing he did that was particularly important was that he made the first full-length feature film ever, and he made it in Hollywood. It was called *The Squaw Man,* and that film drew more people out to California, to Los Angeles, to Hollywood, to make more films."

"So . . . ?"

"So, you weren't listening in class today. Names are *important.* You go to a school named after the guy who practically *founded* Hollywood. You might want to catch a movie or a TV program now and then. You know, to fit in? Think about it."

Dash chucked the rest of his lunch into the garbage can and headed toward the classroom. I would've followed him, but a huge kid blocked my path. He was so big and ugly, he had to be part rhinoceros.

"Hey, weirdo," he said. Then he grabbed the back of my underwear and yanked as hard as he could. My first wedgie of the year. News traveled fast at Cecil B. DeMille Elementary.

The new kid (me) was a weirdo.

2
The Force

BY THE TIME I'D GOTTEN BACK TO CLASS, I'd managed to adjust my underwear back into place, but for the rest of the day I could barely concentrate. I knew people were staring at me and whispering about me behind my back. At the end of the school day, Mrs. Samuelson reminded everyone to check the schedule to see when his or her parent was assigned to come to class. The parents were going to make presentations about what they did for a living, as part of the family heritage unit.

"I've squeezed you in on Friday, Mitch," she said, turning to me. "I hope that will give one of your parents enough time to prepare something."

I nodded, but as I scanned the schedule I noticed something disturbing. Everyone's parents seemed to be involved in some aspect of show business. The occupations listed on the first day alone read like movie credits: director, stunt woman, actors (Tangie's parents), writers (Dash's parents), executive producer, and costume designer. Up against this lineup, my dad couldn't compete.

As I mentioned before, my dad studies bugs. That doesn't seem so bad, right? It's not like he's, say, a bank robber. It doesn't seem like something I'd need to hide. But you have no idea. You see, my dad is a specialist, and what he specializes in is cockroaches. He doesn't just like them, he's obsessed with them. That's all he talks about. I've seen him take any topic of conversation—sports, yo-yos, Shakespeare plays, anything!—and turn it into a conversation about cockroaches. That's all I needed, to be known as the weirdo who doesn't watch TV and whose dad worships cockroaches. Sometimes I wish my dad *was* a bank robber. Now that would be awesome.

I decided right then not to tell him about the presentation.

It took about half an hour for me to walk home from school. My mom wasn't going to start her job as a lecturer in American history at UCLA (the University of California, Los Angeles) until the next semester, so she was home, unpacking boxes

. . . and baking! She handed me a plate with a thick slice of macadamia nut cake. Did I mention how much I love her hobby? Then she opened the fridge to get some milk.

"There is something in this fridge that just does not smell right," she murmured, wrinkling her nose as she removed the carton to pour me a glass. "So, how was your first day at school?"

"Not good," I said, popping a big piece of cake in my mouth.

She dropped her smile. "What does that mean?"

"Oh nothing. Just that I don't fit in, I'm considered the class weirdo, I got wedgied by a caveman. . . ."

"Oh." She sat next to me at the table. "That doesn't sound like a very good day. But, you know, I'm sure it will get better. Once the kids get to really know you. . . ."

This is the same speech my mom has given me every single time I've started late at a new school. I know it by heart. The next thing she was going to say was "They'll find out what a truly great kid you are." She really needs to stop making this speech; it doesn't fool anybody anymore.

"Mom. Please stop," I interrupted. "I know what you're going to say. But I have to go through this every time we move! I'm sick of having to make new friends all the time! Why can't we just stay in one place?"

My mom sighed and rested her head in her hand. "I know,

Mitch. I know. It really isn't fair the way your father and I have moved you around so much. But your dad has to go where the work is. That's what professors do. Unless he gets tenure at a university, his job is not secure."

"So are you saying the reason we keep moving is because Dad keeps getting fired?"

"Ah, well . . . it's complicated."

Which was her way of saying she didn't want to talk about it. So I thought of something else to complain about.

"And how come we don't have a TV, anyway?"

"TV? I don't know." She shrugged. "You were just never very interested in it when you were younger. You always liked being outside, running around, reading, exploring . . . and your dad and I tend to read books and magazines to relax. A TV just seemed like an unnecessary expense."

"Well, we need one now," I said.

"I'll think about it," she said, which we all know means no.

"Mom, by any chance, is the reason we keep moving really because Dad's a bank robber?"

My mom frowned, raising an eyebrow. Can't blame me for trying. I pushed myself away from the table and went to my room.

The next day didn't start off very well. There was a kid in the class who hadn't been there the day before sitting in my seat. He had light brown hair, big green eyes, and perfect teeth. He was talking with Brandon like they were good buddies, so I guess he was also a king of the classroom. He didn't seem to notice me standing right in front of him, so I tapped him on the shoulder.

"Sorry, but I think you're in my seat," I said.

"Sorry, but you thought wrong," he said. He turned back to Brandon.

"I was sitting here yesterday," I said, trying again. He turned around again.

"Well, now *I'm* sitting here." He turned back to Brandon.

"I'm just saying, the teacher assigned this seat to me. . . ."

He turned to me with a look of amazement. "Are you still here? What's *wrong* with you?"

The rest of the class had gotten quiet. Mrs. Samuelson had not entered the room yet, and Dash and Skywalker weren't there either. I wasn't sure what to do. From the looks of him I was pretty sure this kid had never been in a fight in his entire life. And frankly, neither had I. But if I backed down now, my reputation would go right in the toilet. And anyway, where else was I supposed to sit, on the floor?

"Hey, Mitch, come over and sit by me." Suddenly Tangie appeared by my side, locking her arm in mine. She gently led me to the empty seat behind her. I was happy to follow. It was as if a fresh breeze had blown through the class. Everyone relaxed.

Dash and Skywalker finally arrived and stopped at the door, sensing that they had just missed something. Skywalker saw the kid sitting in my seat, and his mouth made an "O" shape as he slipped into the seat behind him. Dash slid into his chair just as Mrs. Samuelson walked in. Two seconds later the bell rang. Day number two had begun.

At lunch I found out more about the kid with the big green eyes.

"That's Axel Maxtone," Dash said as soon as we left the class. I didn't say anything. Dash grabbed my arm. "Mitch, you *do* know who Axel Maxtone is, don't you?"

"Should I?"

"Oh for Pete's sake, Mitch! Axel Maxtone. The star of *My Mom's a Mutant.* He played the little kid! You couldn't have missed that! It was on TV for four years!"

I thought for a second. "Oh, yeah," I said. "I think I saw part of it at a friend's house. It looked kind of dumb."

"It *was* dumb. Horrible! Worst sitcom ever."

"If it was so bad, why do people give a hoot about Axel Maxtone?"

"Because he was the *star*! He was the breakout character! He was on the cover of *Entertainment Weekly* four times!"

"But it was a bad show, right?"

"You really don't understand how things work around here, do you?" Dash said incredulously. "It doesn't matter how bad it was! It was a *hit!*"

"So you're telling me that because he was the star of a hit show, even though it was a horrible show, he's allowed to act like a jerk for the rest of his life?"

"Exactly. Don't try to make any sense of it, just accept it, stay out of his way, and move on."

I learned a lot more about Hollywood that afternoon during the parent presentations. I learned that Dash's dad won an Academy Award, an Oscar, for writing. I learned that Tangie's mom donates half of her salary from each of her movies to a nonprofit organization dedicated to stopping hunger worldwide. I learned that Brandon's dad flies his own plane, plays polo, and collects vintage motorcycles.

But that wasn't all. Each parent who spoke that afternoon had fascinating stories to tell: about famous people, about making dreams come to life, about being part of the most glamorous, exciting business on the planet—the entertainment industry. Even their worst problems sounded fun. Some people said they had to work through the night to meet deadlines, others had to deal with the hot tempers and unreasonable demands of movie stars, and others had to come up with creative solutions to make seemingly impossible situations work. One person worked in freezing weather in the arctic tundra for two weeks just to shoot one scene of a movie. It sounded awesome.

I was so glad my dad wasn't coming in to speak.

The day ended with Axel Maxtone's mother, who was a casting director. She explained that it was her job to know every actor who is out there so that whenever she casts a movie or a television show, she knows right away who would be perfect for each part and who to bring in for an audition.

"I'm on the phone with stars and their agents all the time," she said, "but the thing I like most about my job is discovering a fresh, new face. At least twice a year my colleagues and I hold talent searches. We invite people of all ages, with no prior experience in show business, to come out and audition. It's very exciting because we never know what we might find. Some people have natural talent, or an appealing look, and they don't even know it."

She handed out a flyer for the next talent search, which was going to take place at the Beachwood Park Recreation Center that Saturday.

After school I walked home with Skywalker, who, it

turned out, lived only a couple of blocks away from me. His house was one of the oldest on the block; it looked like a small Mediterranean castle.

"This used to be Charlie Chaplin's house back in the day," he said as he unlocked the front door and waved me in.

As I walked through the door, I was met by a bloated head with one eyeball swinging from its socket. I yelled like crazy, trying to avoid the thick tongue, oozing with warts, flopping out at me. The next thing I knew I was on the floor. I'd tripped over a huge brain with crab legs poking out of it! Then something heavy fell on my shoulder and I yelled again, but it was just Skywalker's hand, and he was laughing his head off.

"Don't be mad," he said, helping me up. "That's our homemade burglar alarm."

I wasn't mad. I was just happy I hadn't wet myself. "What *is* all this stuff?!" I gasped, my heart pumping like crazy.

"Didn't I tell you?" Skywalker chuckled. "My dad's a makeup artist. He creates monsters."

"You actually live in the middle of all this stuff?" I scanned the room. Aliens, vampires, werewolves, and all kinds of gruesome creatures lurked in the shadows, peered out of doorways, and crouched on shelves.

"In October we do. We're setting up for Halloween,"

Skywalker explained with a wicked grin. "This is nothing. Wait till it's finished!"

He led me into the kitchen, which thankfully was not decorated for Halloween, and pulled a couple of popsicles out of the freezer. As he handed me one he was still grinning from ear to ear, like he had some kind of big secret.

"Got a couple of hours to kill?" he asked.

I checked my watch. "Sure, but I should call my mom."

"Do it," he said, handing me his cell phone. "Tell her you're doing some homework."

"I don't remember getting any homework," I said, dialing my number. When my mom answered I told her I was at a friend's house and that we were doing homework and I would be home around six.

Skywalker had finished his popsicle and was pacing around the room, running his fingers through his hair. After I hung up he clapped his hands together. "You ready?"

"Yeah . . . ready for what?"

"Follow me!"

Skywalker led me into a dark room and flicked on the lights. On one wall was a floor-to-ceiling bookcase filled with DVDs and stacks of electronic equipment. Against the second wall were three rows of comfy, theater-style seats. A white screen took up most of the third wall. It was a little movie theater, right in his house! Skywalker pulled a DVD box set from the case and held it up as though it were the crown jewels of England.

"Your homework," he said. "I have here in my hands the complete *Star Wars* deluxe box set, director's cut, in widescreen. Today we will watch the first one ever made. Episode four, *A New Hope*."

"It starts with episode four?"

"Yes. There are two trilogies. The first trilogy had episodes four, five, and six. Then George Lucas—he's the director— went back and made a prequel trilogy of episodes one, two, and three. There are different opinions as to which movie is the best, but I like the first one. So does my dad. He was a teenager when it came out, and it was like nothing he'd ever seen before. He said it changed his life. And now you will see why. Sit."

I sat in one of the theater chairs. Skywalker slid the DVD into the player. The lights dimmed. After a moment, white words came up on the black screen: "A long time ago, in a galaxy far, far away . . ." And then, with a sudden burst of music, the words "Star Wars" appeared over a field of stars.

Two hours later, as the credits started to roll, I blinked and realized that I was still in Skywalker's house, still sitting in his mini-theater. I felt like I'd gone away on a long trip. I couldn't move. I didn't want to leave. I wanted to go back into *Star Wars*. I wanted to hang out with Luke Skywalker and Han Solo. I was aching to take one more jump into hyperspace, desperate to fight one last battle against the evil empire.

"So? What do you think?" Skywalker asked.

"May the Force be with you," I said solemnly. I was hooked.

We were so psyched about the movie that we decided to make a couple of light sabers. We went on a hunt for broomsticks and ended up finding them in Skywalker's bedroom, which, I have to say, was like walking into crazy town.

The whole room was an art project. There were strange mobiles hanging from his ceiling—one made out of an old radio that had been taken apart, one made out of plastic puppet heads, and one made out of candy wrappers that had been wrapped around blocks of wood. He had a lamp made out of an umbrella. He'd strung little white Christmas lights along walls. And there was a mural on one of his walls that was like nothing I'd ever seen before. He noticed me looking at it.

"I painted that," he said proudly. It was a picture of a long line of businessmen and -women with various animal heads, all heading into a flying saucer. Meanwhile, wedges of cheese with wings flew around the sky. I was impressed. All I can draw are stick figures, an apple, and a pretty lame-looking horse.

"What is it?" I asked.

He scrutinized it for a moment. "I don't know. It's not finished yet."

After we found the broomsticks and made our light sabers, we realized there wasn't enough space in his room to battle, so we headed out to his backyard. It occurred to me as I stood at one end of the grass that we probably looked like a couple of first-class dopes, but I forgot all about that when Skywalker charged me head-on. I fended off wave after wave of attacks. Skywalker was really good, twirling, jabbing, jumping, whacking; it was obvious that this was not the first time he'd done this.

Then his mom stuck her head out the window. "Hey, guys, you might want to wind things up. I'll have dinner ready in ten minutes."

I hadn't even known she was home. I dropped my light saber—or rather, my broomstick—totally embarrassed. That gave Skywalker an easy shot at my legs.

"Ouch!"

"Why didn't you jump?"

"I don't want to do this in front of your mom. She's going to think we're a couple of idiots."

Skywalker laughed. "First of all, my mom's known me all my life and has already decided whether or not I'm an idiot, and second, who cares what people think?"

Boy, he and I couldn't be more different. It's a miracle we were friends.

I got home twenty minutes late. My mom pretended to be upset, but she was thrilled I'd made a friend, and so was my dad, so they accepted my apology pretty quickly. Over dinner I told my parents all about my visit with Skywalker: about his fantastic house, the monsters all over the place, his crazy bedroom, and watching *Star Wars* in their private screening room. I left out the part about the broomstick battle.

"Ooh, *Star Wars*. That was such a fun movie! I was a teenager when that came out," my mom said with a laugh.

"I never got into that fantasy stuff," my dad said. "You can find just as much adventure in real life. Battling an evil empire is nothing compared with battling a colony of cockroaches. Now that's a fight! They are practically undefeatable!"

I started to clear my plate from the dinner table, but my dad stopped me. "Wait, Mitch, there was something I wanted to tell you. I received an e-mail from your teacher, Mrs. Samuelson."

I froze. "Really? What did she want?"

"She asked if I could come in tomorrow and make a presentation to the class about my work."

Rats! Rats! Rats! I thought, but I said, "Oh, yeah. I guess I forgot to ask you about that. You know, you don't have to come. I figured you must be pretty busy. . . ."

"Actually I'm free tomorrow afternoon. I told her I could be there at two."

Rats! "You know, you really don't have to. She'll understand. . . ."

"Nonsense! I'm actually looking forward to it. I've never spoken to a grade-school class before!" He seemed way too excited about this.

"Dad, just make sure you keep it short. The short presentations are always better than the long ones."

"Oh, I've got some ideas," my dad said, rubbing his hands together like some kind of mad scientist. *Rats!*

The next day I left for school with a sinking feeling in my stomach. All day I prayed for a meteor to fall from the sky and land in front of the school so that class would be canceled.

When I checked out the list of parents coming in to speak that day, my hopes were lifted. The list included a real estate agent, a prison guard, and my father. No cool show-business jobs, just regular people. Or so I thought. It turned out the real estate agent specialized in multimillion-dollar homes, and she had clients who were some of the biggest celebrities in the entertainment industry. She'd bought and sold homes for sports stars, rock stars, movie stars, and television stars.

"In fact, I was just on my way to show a client a listing," she said, her eyes sparkling. "He agreed to let me drop by here first. He was supposed to stay in the car, but I can see he's itching to come in. . . ."

She opened the classroom door and in walked Monty Montgomery. I didn't recognize him, of course. He just looked like a weird guy with bushy eyebrows and nostrils big enough to hold a couple of eggs, but everyone else in the class knew who he was. They all jumped up and crowded around him. It took ten minutes for Mrs. Samuelson to restore order to the classroom, but everyone got an autograph.

After the real estate agent left, the prison guard came in. He looked pretty rough. He had a broken nose and a scar that stretched from his eye to the back of his neck. He was really giving me the creeps, but I could hear kids around me snickering.

"You think this is funny?" the prison guard shouted, slamming his hand on Brandon's desk. Then he leaned toward Brandon, only inches away from his face.

"Don't cross me, blondie," he growled. "I've eaten bigger things than you for breakfast."

By then everyone was outright laughing. I looked at the sheet and noticed that the prison guard's name was Mr. Bernard Ortega. Skywalker's dad. Now I got it—he was in makeup.

Sure enough, after a few more threats the prison guard finally pointed at his face and said, "You think this mug is ugly? I'm going to show you something really grotesque."

He started to peel off his face. It was the strangest thing I'd ever seen—his face came right off like a rubber mask, and underneath was a middle-aged man who looked like an older version of Skywalker, but with short, gray hair and a mustache.

"I'm going to be picking rubber out of my mustache for days." He laughed, rubbing his face. "Good afternoon, everyone. I'm Bernie Ortega, Skywalker's pop. I'm going to talk to you a little bit about the magic of makeup."

Mr. Ortega had brought in a PowerPoint presentation of the mask-making process, as well as a plaster cast of his own face. He explained that he'd sculpted the guard face right onto the plaster cast. From that he'd made a mold, and from that he'd made a latex appliance, which he then painted. He told us that sometimes he'd make separate latex pieces and glue them to an actor's face in sections, but that other times he'd make a full mask.

"Separate pieces look more realistic because they can

move more naturally with the facial muscles," he explained. "But it takes a lot longer to put them on. Sometimes, if a character only has a bit part or is only going to be visible in the background, it's cheaper and faster to go with the mask."

By the time he left I had forgotten what was coming up, but then Mrs. Samuelson put on a big smile and said, "Our last presenter today is Mr. Mathis."

Then my dad came in. He was in costume too.

My father was dressed like a cockroach.

3

The New Me

THIS WOULD'VE BEEN A GOOD TIME FOR that meteor to show up. A fiery explosion leaving a huge, smoking crater in front of the school was about the only thing that could've saved me. It's too painful for me to describe what happened next, but in case you find yourself in a similar situation, here is a list to give to your parents before they come to school to give a presentation:

RULES FOR PARENT PRESENTATIONS

1. No cockroach costumes.
2. Don't use the Latin name for everything.
3. If you have a bug collection, bring the dead ones pinned to Styrofoam, not live ones in a jar.
4. Don't accidentally drop your live cockroaches.

By the end of the day I had a new nickname: Roach Boy. I didn't care for it.

"Is your teacher mad at me?" my dad asked over dinner.

"I wouldn't call it mad, exactly," I said, "but I don't think she wants you to come back any time soon."

"You tried too hard," my mom said, putting a hand on my dad's shoulder. "I'm sure it'll be all right." She said that because she's married to him, so it's her job to say things like that. But her eyes were saying, "What the heck were you thinking?!"

"Well, I did manage to get most of the roaches back in the jar," my dad said.

How could he not know that "most" is not enough?

"Are we going to move to another town soon?" I said hopefully.

"Don't be silly. We just got here," my mom said.

"Hey, it's Friday," my dad added. "By Monday nobody's even going to remember it happened."

I excused myself and went to my room.

I threw myself on my bed and screamed into my pillow. Bandit jumped on my bed and started licking my face, so I had to stop. My mom and dad clearly didn't get it. This was the worst introduction to a school that I'd ever had. I'd become the enemy of the king of the classroom, everyone thought I was weirdo, and now, on top of all that, I was Roach Boy. All I could think of was the lifetime of wedgies awaiting me. I thought about stopping wearing underwear altogether.

There had to be some way out of this, some way to turn things around. . . . Then I remembered something.

I searched through my backpack and found a piece of paper wadded up under my science book: the casting-call flyer. Axel Maxtone was king of the classroom. Why? *Because he had been on television.* Even though he was on it two years ago, and it was a terrible show, he was still considered supercool.

I needed that kind of cool.

I called up Skywalker.

"I need help," I said.

"You're telling me."

"Seriously. Can you help me get ready for this casting call this weekend?"

There was silence on the other end of the line for a few seconds. "Uh, Mitch, you do know that the chances of your being picked to be in anything are really, really low. It's like winning the lottery. A one-in-a-million shot."

"Yeah, but people *do* win the lottery sometimes, and the only way you can win is to buy a ticket."

"Well, you've got a point there."

"I need to do something," I said. "You saw what happened today."

I heard muffled laughter on the other line. "Okay, okay, I'll help you. You're obviously desperate. Let me see . . ." Then suddenly I detected a slight change in his voice, like the electricity had turned on, starting up his engine. "Okay, you'll need a résumé and a head shot—that's an eight-by-ten photo of yourself. Be at my house at nine, and wear a striped shirt if you have one. Don't worry, this is going to be great. Man, I love a good project!"

The next morning I was at Skywalker's house wearing a red-and-white-striped shirt.

"Excellent!" Skywalker said, rubbing his hands together. "I've got my dad's digital camera—let's take some snapshots. Outside lighting looks the best."

"Why the striped shirt?" I asked, following him outside.

"It's all-American," he said. "You need an 'image,' you know what I mean? When people look at your eight-by-ten, it has to immediately make them think of something. The first time I laid eyes on you I thought, *all-American.* With those freckles, the messed-up hair, the snaggletooth, you look really goofy."

"You think *I'm* the one who looks goofy? You look like what would happen if Dracula and an elf had a baby."

Skywalker just grinned. "Hey, I'm one of a kind, bro. An

original. Besides, goofy's good! How many classy, sophisticated roles do you think there are for kids our age? None, that's how many." He pointed to a tree in the front yard. "Stand over there."

I did. Skywalker walked around me, snapping pictures from different angles while he kept on talking. "You're a farm boy, Mitch. Huck Finn. You're all about cornfields and lazy rivers, vagabonds riding the rails to see the countryside, newsboys hawking newspapers. . . . You like nothing better than shooting marbles, spinning tops, and bouncing yo-yos, and you've got frogs and gum and a slingshot in your pockets. Now smile and show off that crazy tooth of yours. That tooth is your ticket, baby!"

I smiled hard, perhaps a little too hard. Just then Dash rode up on his bike, carrying a satchel. "What's wrong with you? You look like you're constipated," he said.

"I suppose you came here to make fun of me."

"On the contrary," Dash said, "I'm here to help. I heard you needed a résumé." He opened up his satchel and lifted out a laptop computer.

"Dash is an awesome writer," Skywalker said. "I thought he might be able to, you know, make you sound a little . . . give you some . . . dress up your . . ."

"He wants me to make you sound better than you are.

40

And I have to say, this will be a nearly impossible assignment, but I'm up for the challenge," Dash said with a wry grin.

"Thanks a lot."

"Let's start from the beginning," Dash said, ignoring my sarcasm. He opened the laptop and cracked his knuckles. "Name, address, and person to contact . . . You don't happen to have an agent, do you?"

"Come on, Dash, you think anyone would be representing this guy in a billion years?" Skywalker said. Then he quickly added, "Er, no offense, Mitch."

"I'm just trying to make it look professional," Dash said, starting to set up the page. "Casting directors don't really take you seriously if you don't have an agent."

"But Axel's mom said they were looking for fresh, new faces. Doesn't that mean people with no experience, and therefore, no agent?"

"Well, yes and no. Casting directors *say* they love discovering someone fresh and new, but they only trust their opinion if the person has already been discovered by somebody else, like an agent."

"That doesn't make sense."

"There are a lot of things in Hollywood that don't make sense. Just accept it and move on."

I scratched my head. "Okay, then how do you get an agent?"

"Most agents don't trust their instincts either, so the best way to get an agent is to get an acting job first."

"Didn't you just say you need the agent to get the acting job in the first place?"

"Yes."

I started to protest, but Dash held up his hand before I could say anything.

"Accept it and move on." Dash turned back to his computer. "We need a list of your credits. Have you appeared in any movies, television shows, or plays?"

"Not really."

"Come on. Work with me here. Think harder."

I thought harder.

"Well, I was on the news once for a tree-planting project my class did in New Haven, and I was visible for a split second at the Macy's Thanksgiving Day parade," I offered.

Dash started typing. "What else?"

"I was in the Christmas pageant at my school in Seattle and in a different one in St. Paul. The first was just a bunch of holiday songs, but the second was the story of Rudolph the Red-Nosed Reindeer."

"Good, good. What did you play?"

"I was a cloud."

He stopped typing. "A what?"

"A cloud. You know, 'Then one foggy Christmas Eve, Santa came to say . . .' I was part of the fog. Also my family takes home-video movies on our vacations, like when we went to Yellowstone Park and it rained the whole time, or when we visited the Statue of Liberty, and I'm pretty sure my parents have a video of when I was born."

Dash started typing again. "Name some of your hobbies."

"I like making lists, hiking, science experiments, magic tricks, building stuff, baseball, ice hockey, jujitsu, handball, basketball, football, snowboarding, skateboarding. . . ."

"How about any special skills?"

"I can juggle, ride a unicycle, play piano and guitar, and I know sign language."

Dash stopped typing again and looked up at me. "You sure know how to do a lot of stuff."

I shrugged. "I don't have a TV. I have to do something."

Skywalker looked at the list. "You play guitar? I play drums, and Dash plays keyboard. We were thinking of starting a band last year, but it kinda fell apart. . . ."

"Focus, Skywalker," Dash snapped, suddenly irritated. "That's ancient history." Dash typed a few more words and then stopped.

"I'm finished." He turned his computer for me to see, and this is what I saw:

MATHIS MITCHELL

(310) 555-6767

P.O. Box 1200 · Hollywood, CA 90028

Movies

Bad Day at Yellowstone	Independent film	Young Boy
Lady Liberty	Independent film	Son
The Birth of Roach Boy	Independent film	Roach Boy

Television

The Day the Trees Took Root	Documentary	Planter
A Day of Thanks	Documentary	Boy

Plays

Rudolph the Red-Nosed Reindeer	The Evil Fog
Christmas Extravaganza, Live!	Chorus

Special Skills & Interests

Circus tricks (juggling, gymnastics, unicycle, stilts),

ice skating, skateboarding, equestrian, team sports, hiking,

magic, science, building and architecture, piano, guitar,

strong organizational skills

"Wow, this is great," I said. "But how come you switched my name around?"

"It's sounds better. Actors change their names all the time."

"That's true," Skywalker chimed in. "Did you know Axel's real name is Alex? And Maxtone is just something his mom made up—her last name is Mulligan."

"Well, I really prefer Mitch," I said.

"Yeah, it's more 'all-American,'" Skywalker agreed. "Change it back."

Dash shrugged and made the fix.

"Just one more thing," I added. "Please take out the Roach Boy reference."

"Oh, you caught that?" Dash chuckled.

"Yeah. I caught it. Just take it out."

Dash did and then saved the résumé on his computer.

"Let's print this out. We've only got a few minutes before the casting call starts," Skywalker said, heading into his house.

"But the casting session lasts for three hours," I said. "There's plenty of time."

"You want to get there early," Skywalker said. "Trust me."

4

Like a Bunch of Cattle

WE REACHED THE RECREATION CENTER ten minutes after twelve, and the line was already out the door and around the block. There had to be at least three hundred people there, maybe more.

Dash saved a spot at the end of the line while Skywalker and I searched for the check-in table. When we found it we had to stand in a whole other line, not as long as the first. It took about ten minutes to get to the front. A young woman with large glasses smiled at me as I stepped up to the table.

"Mitch Mathis," I said. "I'm signing in."

"All right," she said. "Ah, I'm sorry, do you have a parent here? Or a guardian?"

"Oh . . . uh . . . she's . . . my mom's waiting in the other line," I lied. "She didn't know she had to check in with me. I really don't want her to lose her place. . . ."

The woman nodded sympathetically. "I understand," she said. "Just take this waiver and give it to her to sign. You can hand it in to the casting director when you're called."

"Thank you," I said, taking the paper.

"Do you have a head shot and résumé?" She glanced at what I had brought. "Very good. No, no, don't give it to me, keep it with you and hand it to the casting director when you meet her."

Skywalker and I left to look for Dash at the end of the long line.

"That was pretty good," Skywalker said. "You're a natural."

"A natural liar?" I said.

"Lying, acting . . . it's all the same." He signed my waiver for me.

We found Dash sitting on the sidewalk. There were already thirty people behind him in the line, so I was glad he had saved a spot for us.

"Don't despair, the line's moving quickly."

Dash must think snails move quickly, because it took us an hour to reach the building.

While we were waiting we played Twenty Questions, I Spy, and Rock Paper Scissors, and then we stamped on each other's feet just for the heck of it. I taught them three easy magic tricks. We threw rocks at a fire hydrant. Then we ran out of things to do. We were just about to start stamping on each other's feet again when Tangie and J.J. rode up on their bicycles. As much as J.J. pretended to be annoyed by Tangie, they seemed to hang out a lot.

"Hi," J.J. said. "What are you guys doing here?"

"Growing old," Skywalker said.

"Having an unbearable amount of fun," Dash said.

"Mitch? Don't you have a sarcastic answer?" J.J. asked.

"Huh? Uh, no." I wasn't really paying attention to J.J.; Tangie was drawing her fingers through her hair. She had a dimple in her cheek when she smiled.

J.J. squinted her eyes. "Hey, wait a minute. This isn't the cattle call, is it? The casting session Mrs. Mulligan was talking about?"

Busted. Now that Big Mouth figured it out, everyone would know. I decided to just go ahead and admit it.

"Yeah, I thought I'd give it a shot. It sounded like fun."

J.J. shrugged. "Okay, if you say so."

"Why do you want to be an actor?" Tangie asked, the same way you might say, "Why do you want to be a garbage man?" She really was out of it. Cute—but out of it.

I wasn't about to explain the real reason, so I just said, "Hey, doesn't everybody want to be a star?"

"But we're already stars," she answered. "Everything that exists is made up of the stars, exploding out of that first big bang that created the universe."

I didn't know how to respond to that exactly, so I tried to change the subject. "Both of your parents are actors, right? Do you have any advice? I've never done anything like this before."

"Sure. Forget everything."

"Forget . . . everything?"

"That's right. Don't act. Be natural. Be in the moment. Be genuine. Just . . . be."

"That's supposed to help me impress these casting directors? That's your best acting advice?"

Tangie smiled. "Not acting advice, just . . . advice."

"Oh for heaven's sake, Tangie, say something useful!" J.J. snapped. "Here's some real advice, Mitch. Don't worry about impressing them. When you go in there, pretend you don't care how well you do."

"Won't that just make the casting directors mad at me for wasting their time?"

"Oh, no, just the opposite. If they think you don't want what they're offering, they'll be desperate to have you. Trust me."

"She's absolutely right about that," Dash said.

"But that doesn't make any sense," I protested.

"Nevertheless, it is accurate. Accept it and . . ."

"I know, I know, 'move on,'" I finished for him.

"Speaking of moving on, we've got to go," J.J. said. "Have fun waiting in line."

"Break a leg, Mitch," Tangie added as they mounted their bikes and rode off.

"'Break a leg'? I've always wondered why people say that," I said after they'd gone.

"It's a theater superstition. It's bad luck to wish someone good luck," Skywalker explained. "So you wish them something bad, like a broken leg."

Before I could respond to that, Dash held up his hand. I knew what he was going to say, so we said it together: "Accept it and move on!"

Twenty minutes dragged by as we edged closer to the door. Ahead of me a young man counted people in line as he let them pass into the recreation center. Just as we reached him he stopped the line.

"Hold on," he said. "Are all of you auditioning?"

"No, just me," I answered.

"Forty-five," he counted, shooing me in. He turned to Skywalker and Dash. "Sorry, guys, no looky-loos. Parents only."

"Mitch, do you want us to wait for you?" Dash said.

"No, I don't know how long it's going to take," I said. "I'll call you later."

"Okay. See you. Break a leg."

"Yeah. Multiple fractures," Skywalker added.

Once inside, the larger group of forty-five was split into three groups of fifteen. One group was led to the stage in the back of the room, which had been curtained off. Another group was led to a small gym that was used for yoga classes and senior citizens' activities. My group passed both of these areas and was led to the children's playroom. I could tell it was the children's playroom because through the little window in the door I could see some large foam pads, balls, toy instruments, and cardboard blocks stacked in the corner. There was a table set up, and behind it sat Axel Maxtone's mother.

The girl who led us to the room took our paperwork and went inside. We all chose a seat on the benches along the wall outside the room. The kids in my group ranged in age from six years old to a guy who looked like he needed a shave. For the first time I noticed that I was the only one who came by myself. Everyone else had a mom, and their moms were coaching them.

"Bright eyes!" I heard one big lady say to her daughter as she tucked in her shirt. "Eyes wide open! Energy! Energy!"

"Make sure to greet everyone in the room," I heard another lady mutter under her breath. "Remember to thank them afterward."

One girl about my age looked pretty miserable. Her mother was yanking her tightly by the wrist.

"I can't believe you wore that awful shirt!" the mom hissed.

"It's my lucky shirt. . . ."

"It's a rag! If I had known that's what you had on under your jacket, I wouldn't have even brought you here! Look, just . . . just keep the jacket on. As soon as we get home I'm throwing that ugly shirt right in the garbage!"

I turned away. I was glad I was by myself. My mom wouldn't be like these moms, but still, I was glad not to have anyone fussing over me.

The young woman came out of the playroom and called the first kid's name. A dark-haired boy about nine years old leaped up and followed her inside. His mother stayed in the hall. Through the window I could see him approach Axel's mom at the table. Mrs. Mulligan talked to him and then handed him something, which he read. They talked some more, and then she laughed. Then they talked some more, and then he started to sing.

I didn't know we were going to have to sing! That was bad news. I'm not much of a singer. There's a reason I was cast as the fog in *Rudolph the Red-Nosed Reindeer*. Skywalker's words of warning began to sink in. This really was a long shot. I was a fool to think this talent search could solve my problems.

I glanced around for the nearest exit. I could pretend to have to go to the bathroom and then never come back.

The first kid came out, and he had a big, broad smile on his face.

"Sophie Westin?" the young woman called out. In went Sophie, the girl with the mean mom and the raggedy shirt. She didn't do very well. I could see her through the window, hanging her head. She looked scared. She didn't sing anything. Out she came, and her mom whisked her away.

"Mitch Mathis? Is there a Mitch Mathis here?"

I was so caught up with that girl and her problems, I'd totally forgotten that I was going to bolt. Now it was too late; I had to go in. "Here I am," I said, raising my hand.

"Follow me," she said.

Axel's mom remembered me from her classroom presentation, which surprised me, and I told her so.

"I have a good eye for faces," she explained. "It helps when you're a casting director to be able to remember people. And you have a . . . memorable face." I knew what she meant. Goofy.

She glanced at my résumé, frowning every once in a while.

"Did you make this stuff up?" she said finally.

"Er . . . no . . . ," I lied. Well, it wasn't really a lie; Dash was the one who made it up.

"You're telling me you can juggle, walk on stilts, ride a unicycle, do a flip in the air. . . ."

"Oh! Yeah!" I said, almost laughing, I was so relieved. I thought she was going to nail me on the phony credits.

"Show me." She leaned back in the chair and crossed her arms. She didn't believe me. Suddenly I didn't like her very much. I know I lie sometimes, but I can't stand it when somebody doesn't believe me.

I grabbed three rubber balls from the bin and started juggling. I kept them in the air in a tight circle, and then I made the circle wider and higher. When I added a fourth ball, Mrs. Mulligan's eyes nearly popped out of her head. I whipped the balls between my legs and over my shoulder, and for my finale I caught three balls and spun around to catch the fourth.

That turned out to be a mistake. As I was spinning, Axel came into the room.

"Hey, Roach Boy!" he yelled.

That threw me off. My hand hit one of the balls, sending it flying across the room. It popped Axel's mom right in the forehead.

"Ow!" she said.

"Hey, what do you think you're doing, jerk! That's my mom!" Axel raced over to me and shoved me in the chest. It wasn't much of a shove, but I tripped on the balls I'd dropped and fell over.

"Axel, stop it!" his mother barked, rubbing her forehead. "I'm fine. What do you want?"

"I need money for lunch."

"Get it from Hillary. She's in the gym."

Axel nodded and skulked out, but not before he glared at me with a look that said, *Watch out kid, you're dead meat.*

"Let's get back to this," Axel's mom said. She had a round, purple spot where the ball had hit her. "Can you sing?"

"Yes, but badly."

"So that means no," she said pointedly. "How about a joke?"

I knew a lot of jokes, but most of them were not good ones to share with adults. Many involved toilets.

She looked up from her list. "Well?"

My mind grasped for the something . . . anything . . . "Er . . . what's brown and sticky?"

She narrowed her eyes at me. "I give up," she said evenly. "Tell me. What exactly *is* brown and sticky?"

I gulped. "A stick. Heh-heh-heh . . . get it?"

She frowned. "A stick?"

"Yeah, a stick is brown and stick-y. Stick-y. As in, 'like a stick.'" You know you're in trouble if you have to explain the joke.

"Thank you very much, Mitch. We'll let you know if we find anything that's right for you."

No she wouldn't. I was a much better liar than she was.

"Thanks for your time, Mrs. Mulligan," I said.

"It was my pleasure," she muttered, without looking up.

By the time I got home, I had figured out a whole new plan to solve my problem. "I was thinking that I would like to go to military school," I announced over dinner.

My mom nearly choked on her carrots. "Why on earth would you want to go to military school?"

"It would give structure to my life—you know, build character."

"Mitch, most military schools are boarding schools. You'd have to live somewhere else," my dad said.

"I know, but it might be an eye-opening experience. Broaden my horizons."

"Why do you sound like a recruitment pamphlet?" my mom said. "Who have you been talking to anyway? What have you been up to?"

"Take it easy, Helen, I'll handle this," my dad said, putting his hand on her arm. He turned to me. "Mitch, who have you been talking to? What have you been up to?"

"Forget it," I said. "I was just kidding." I stuffed the last few forkfuls of chicken in my mouth. "May I please be excused?"

Just then the phone rang. That would be Skywalker, wondering what had happened at the talent search. I'd forgotten to call him. I didn't want to talk to him in front of my parents, so I grabbed my plate and headed into the kitchen.

"If that's Skywalker, let him know I'll call him back after I finish the dishes," I yelled back. I started rinsing off the pots and pans that were already in the sink. After a few minutes my mom and dad both came into the kitchen. My dad leaned against the doorway, his arms crossed. My mom's arms were crossed too. That wasn't a good sign.

"Mitch, that was a Mrs. Mulligan on the phone. Is there something you'd like to tell us?" my dad said calmly, his voice a little higher than usual. That *really* wasn't a good sign.

At moments like this, there's only one thing you can do. Tell the truth.

"I went to a talent search today," I admitted. "I was with Skywalker, like I said I'd be, but we went to the recreation center. Mrs. Mulligan was the casting director. I juggled for her and accidentally knocked her in the head with a ball. She may have been hurt, just a tiny bit, but it was an accident!"

"Thank you for telling the truth," my father said, his voice back to normal.

"Is she suing us?" I asked. "Because she was totally conscious and alert when I left the room."

"Uh, no, she's not suing us," my mom said. "She wants you to go to Warner Brothers Studios in Burbank on Monday morning for a commercial audition."

I was stunned. "You're . . . you're kidding," I said finally. "She hated my guts."

"Well, apparently she liked something about you. I'm not sure how we feel about it, though, considering this is the first we've heard of it."

I took a deep breath and explained what had been going on at school, how I needed to turn my reputation around, and why I had gone to the talent search. I was careful to not mention my dad's role in all of this, though it wasn't easy. I think he guessed anyway, because he looked a little guilty.

"Mitch, is this something you really want to do?" my mother said, looking concerned. "You've never been interested in drama or acting before."

"Yes! Mom, this would really help a lot," I said.

"You may think it will, Mitch, but becoming an actor is no way to make real friends. Besides, we don't know anything about show business! We won't be able to give you any advice at all. And I don't like the idea of your missing school. You should be settling into this house, getting to know the community. . . ."

You know how you can tell when your parents are winding up to hand you a big, fat NO? That's what this speech was. I had to stop it before the word came out of her mouth. Once the big, fat NO lands on the table, it's almost impossible to get it off. I needed to think up something to stop the arrival of that NO, and fast.

"Mom," I interrupted. "I *am* trying to get to know the community. This is *Hollywood.* Show business *is* the community. So what if it's new to us? You've always said that I shouldn't be afraid to try new things, and that it's important to have new, challenging experiences. What is that poem you keep quoting by Robert Frost? 'Two roads diverged in a wood, and I—I took the one less traveled by, and that has made all the difference.' That's what I'm doing. This is the road less traveled by. I promise I won't let it affect my schoolwork. Besides, it's just an audition. I probably won't get the part, but it will be interesting, educational, and fun to try."

My mom was impressed. My dad was impressed. It was the poetry that did it.

WAYS TO IMPRESS YOUR PARENTS

1. Quote poetry.
2. Ask how their day was, then listen to the answer without interrupting.
3. When meeting one of their friends, shake their hand and say clearly, "A pleasure to meet you, sir [or ma'am]."
4. Read the news part of the newspaper.
5. Write thank-you notes. Use real stationery, not e-mail.
6. Remember their birthdays and their wedding anniversary.
7. Clean up a mess THEY made.

"All right, Mitch," my dad said. "Give it a shot. But you have to make up any work that you've missed. I expect A's out of you. If your grades drop, it's over."

"I promise," I said.

"I'll call that lady back," my mom said, and then she added, "I don't know if you're a good actor, but you'd sure make a good lawyer."

I smiled. I couldn't wait to call Skywalker and Dash.

I didn't know everything was about to change. Forever.

5
You Like Bubbles?

I CALLED SKYWALKER FIRST. HE WAS really excited, almost more excited than I was.

"This is huge!" Skywalker said. *"You're the one kid in a million!"*

"I don't have the part yet," I reminded him.

"Oh, you can forget about that, that's a hopeless dream for you."

"But you just said I was the one kid in a million."

"But actually *getting* the part, that's one in, like, five million."

"Where are you getting these numbers? I think you're making them up."

"Well, yeah, I am. But seriously, don't get your hopes up."

"Okay, but don't tell anyone about it. I don't want anyone to know about it if I don't get it."

"Don't worry, I won't say anything, 'cause you're not going to get it. Have fun fantasizing about it, though." He hung up.

Dash actually had some advice. His father had been in casting sessions before and had told Dash some of the mistakes actors make when they come in for an audition.

WHAT TO DO IN AN AUDITION

1. Don't be late.
2. Be prepared. Know the role.
3. If you come in costume, don't overdo it. (Example: no cockroach costume.)
4. Don't ignore or insult the receptionist, secretary, or anyone else you meet on your way in; they talk about you after you leave and it gets back to the writer, director, and producer.
5. Be upbeat and enthusiastic, but not so much that you appear insane. Try to make them laugh.
6. Don't criticize the script or ask if you can change your lines; the writer may be in the room and doesn't want your notes.

7. Don't bring bribes or gifts, but do have an interesting story to tell about yourself so that they will remember you.

8. Do it right the first time—first impressions are everything. Don't bump into the furniture.

9. When you're finished, look them in the eye and thank them for seeing you. Last impressions are also everything.

10. Above all, BE NATURAL.

At nine thirty, while I was getting ready for bed, the doorbell rang. My parents usually don't answer the door after eight in the evening unless they're expecting someone, but whoever was at the door was insistent. BING-BONG, BING-BONG, BING-BONG. My father closed his newspaper and cautiously opened the door. It was a young man dressed in regular street clothes. He looked like he was in a hurry.

"May I help you? I'm not going to buy or sign anything," my dad warned.

The man thrust a manila envelope at him. "Sign here please," he said, ignoring what my dad had said about not signing anything.

My dad read the paper on the clipboard and then signed

it. The man thanked him, went back to his car, and drove away. Then my dad looked at the envelope, surprised.

"Mitch, this is for you."

In an instant I was by his side. I ripped open the envelope and pulled out a script. It was very short, only about three pages long. This is what it said on the cover:

FIZZY WHIZ SODA

"You Like Bubbles?"

REVISED SECOND DRAFT

Director: Alvin Fisher

Bieterman, Schwartz,
and VanDyke, Inc.
1200 125th Street
New York, NY 10010

My mom and dad were now hovering over my shoulder as I opened the script to the first page. This is what it said:

```
                 FIZZY WHIZ SODA

               "You Like Bubbles?"


FADE IN:
Music Cue: Hip, up-tempo music.
EXT. BASKETBALL COURT — DAY
We see TWO TEENAGERS in a pickup game,
dribbling, taking shots, etc.
              DEEP VOICE (V.O.)
    Some things should never be flat.
CAMERA PANS to the other side of the
court. We see a SAD BOY trying to
dribble with a FLAT BASKETBALL. CLOSE
UP on his depressed expression.
MONTAGE OVER MUSIC:
1. EXT. NEIGHBORHOOD STREET — DAY
    A group of BOYS AND GIRLS rides
    bikes down the street. One GIRL is
    left in the dust by her friends as
    she struggles to pedal. ANGLE ON
    BICYCLE WHEELS, which are flat.
```

2. INT. KITCHEN/DINING ROOM — EVENING

   A MOM whisks a soufflé out of the oven and carries it to her waiting FAMILY at the dining room table. As soon as she gets to the table, the soufflé collapses. The family frowns; the mom is distressed.

3. EXT. OLD SHIP 1492 — DAY

   CHRISTOPHER COLUMBUS, on his ship, gazes through a spyglass at the ocean's horizon. CAMERA PULLS BACK farther and farther until we are out in SPACE and see the image of PLANET EARTH. CAMERA MOVES around the EARTH, revealing that the earth is actually on a flat plane.

                    CUT TO:

   CHRISTOPHER COLUMBUS as he notices the ocean is pouring over the edge into a huge waterfall. ANGLE ON SPACE POV: The ship goes over the edge of the earth, falling into oblivion.

4. EXT. BASKETBALL COURT — DAY

A BORED BUSINESSMAN, who is watching the pickup game, pops open a can of generic soda, drinks, and is disgusted. He pours the offending drink on the ground.

ANGLE ON: THE FIZZY WHIZ KID weaves in and out of the basketball players on a unicycle and stops in front of the businessman.

> FIZZY WHIZ KID
>
> You like bubbles?

The man nods. The kid reaches into his jacket, which is lined with cans of FIZZY WHIZ SODA. He picks one, pops it open, and hands it to the man, who takes a deep, refreshing drink.

CLOSE ON: The man's eyes. They fill up with flashing sparkles and bubbles! The businessman grabs the basketball, executes some amazing dribbling and fancy footwork, then shoots a basket from mid-court, much to the amazement and applause of the pickup players.

CLOSE ON: FIZZY WHIZ KID, who holds the
soda can up to camera.
CLOSE ON: FIZZY WHIZ SODA CAN
                DEEP VOICE (V.O.)
     Fizzy Whiz Soda. You like bubbles?
CHYRON HUGE LETTERS THAT FILL THE
SCREEN: YOU LIKE BUBBLES?

                            FADE OUT.

There were a lot of things about the script that I didn't understand, but I got the general idea. Somebody had high-lighted the line for the Fizzy Whiz Kid with yellow marker.

"I guess they want me to try out for the part of the Fizzy Whiz Kid," I said.

"It's only one line. That shouldn't be too hard," my dad said.

"Why don't you practice it, Mitch," my mom suggested.

"You like bubbles?" I said. My parents looked at each other, not sure what to do next.

"Well, that sounded good to me," my dad said finally, sitting back on the couch. He picked up the newspaper.

"I guess so," my mom said with a shrug. She reread the cover letter. "This says you need to be at Warner Brothers Studios at nine o'clock. You'd better get some sleep. You don't want to be yawning through the audition."

I took the script and went to my room. I read it a few more times. It did seem easy enough. Maybe I was missing something. I lay back on my pillow and stared at the ceiling. Then I said the line a few more times aloud. I tried to make it sound like I was really excited about the soda. They probably wanted the Fizzy Whiz Kid to be really enthusiastic about the product. I practiced it that way a few more times until I was satisfied, and then snuggled under my blanket and fell asleep.

The next day I skipped breakfast. I was too excited. I had already chewed down my fingernails and picked off two scabs that now required band-aids before we'd even gotten out the door. My mom threatened to make me wear mittens if I didn't stop, so I put a rubber band around my wrist and played with it to keep my fingers busy.

Mom drove me to Warner Bros. Studios in Burbank, which is in an area of Los Angeles known as "the Valley." The Valley refers to the San Fernando Valley, which is on the northern side of the Santa Monica Mountains, which cut through the huge city of Los Angeles.

The first thing I saw as we came out of the mountains was the water tower with the Warner Bros. symbol painted on it.

I could see it poking out from the rest of the studio buildings. That was very exciting. Even though I haven't watched a lot of TV or seen many movies, I still recognized that symbol.

As we continued down the road, we reached one side of the studio lot, which seemed to go on forever. You couldn't see where it ended. The lot was surrounded by a tall wall, and behind the wall were a bunch of wide buildings that were like giant shoe boxes with rounded roofs, all lined up in rows. (I found out later they're called soundstages.)

Farther down the street we started seeing billboards advertising movies and television shows that had been produced by Warner Bros. These billboards were gigantic. It was a little weird seeing twenty-foot-tall faces grinning down at you.

"I always thought actors had big heads," my mom said, trying to be funny—but I could tell she was nervous too. I hoped she would calm down before we got there. My mom gets a little weird when she's nervous.

We drove past one billboard after another until we reached the Gate 3 driveway. One side of the driveway said VISITORS, the other said EMPLOYEES. We took the visitor side.

The guard at the gate leaned out of his guard box. He was in full uniform, which of course didn't help my mom's nervousness. I could see little drops of sweat forming on her forehead.

"Name, please?"

"Helen Mathis."

The guard checked his computer and shook his head. "Would you be under some other name?"

"Ah, well, I'm sure there must be a mistake, ah, I mean, we were instructed to . . ." She was getting that squirrely look, shifting in her seat, like at any moment she would bolt from the car.

I leaned over her to talk to the guard. "Could you please try Mitch Mathis, sir?"

The guard checked again and nodded, and then printed out a pass that he taped to our windshield. He handed my mom a map after tracing a path on it with a highlighter pen.

"You're going to Bungalow Twenty-three," he said. "Just follow the yellow line on the map. You're going to turn left at the stop sign, then straight through the next two stop signs, then make another left, and then a right at this street. Keep going until you get to the parking lot. Go ahead and park in any visitor space. You're going to see three two-story buildings that all look the same. Go into the one that's the third from the right and sign in at the guard desk. He'll tell you where to go from there. Got it?"

"Yes," my mom said. She drove through the gate, happy to be done with him. "You got some of that, didn't you, Mitch?" she said hopefully.

"I think so," I said, but I wasn't sure. We drove past a sea of parked cars and took a left at the first stop sign.

After that we were lost.

6
Don't Bump into the Furniture

WE DROVE AROUND AIMLESSLY, PASSING
one soundstage after another. They seemed to go on forever,
and they all looked pretty much the same on the outside. I
checked the map. It had been copied so many times that the
names of the buildings and the numbers assigned to them were
impossible to read. We would have to stop and ask someone for
directions.

We parked in front of some wooden bungalows
(bungalows again! just like school!) and looked around for
someone to ask—a guard, or a friendly face to approach—
but everyone we saw looked very busy. People in suits walked
by arguing, people in jeans walked by laughing, big dudes
wearing leather tool belts walked by pushing huge trolleys
loaded with electrical equipment, and all kinds of people
buzzed around on golf carts. It was unbelievable how many

golf carts almost ran us over. There were more golf carts here than on a golf course.

My mom grabbed my hand and walked faster.

Racing around a studio lot is sort of like being in a dream, or a nightmare, depending on how you look at it. Every time you turn a corner you're in a whole new world. For instance, we turned a corner and almost bumped into a group of women dressed as daisies. They had big, droopy petals around their heads and wore green, skintight bodysuits. Two of them were smoking while the other was screeching into her cell phone. A man dressed like a watering can stuck his head out of a stage door.

"Break's over, you guys!" he said. The two ladies stubbed out their cigarettes, and the third snapped her phone closed. They straightened their petals and followed him back inside.

We raced by a soundstage that had its door wide open, and I caught a glimpse of the inside, which had been transformed into a treasure cave filled with mountains of gold. Waterfalls trickled down the walls, and the entire floor had been flooded so that there was a lake right in the middle of the stage. If my mother hadn't been with me, I might've skipped the audition altogether and gone in to explore, but she grabbed my arm and dragged me along. We were going to be late.

We turned one corner and suddenly we were in New York,

running past brownstone buildings. There were old metal garbage cans and graffiti on the walls. There was a pawnshop across the street from a newsstand, and an old-fashioned drugstore. All the buildings were empty.

Around the bend we found a little town square with a bandstand in the center of a park. Single-story cottages lined the streets, along with a little church on the corner, and a small movie theater next to a diner. All empty.

We turned another corner, and we were in a ritzy French neighborhood. We raced by cafés, boutiques, and a flower stand, all of which were deserted. It felt like an atomic bomb had cleared the world and we were the only ones left, searching for the Fizzy Whiz audition.

Then around the next corner we stumbled upon a homeless camp. Makeshift tents crowded the sidewalk, and rough-looking people in ragged clothes stood around a garbage can in which they'd lit a fire. I saw a few drinking out of bottles hidden in paper bags. They looked up at us angrily as we walked by, and a few yelled something out at us, but my mom tightened her grip on my wrist and walked even faster.

"Just ignore them," she whispered. "Don't make eye contact."

"But, Mom," I started. "I think this is—"

"Sweetie, I want to help them too, but this isn't the time."

She shuddered and muttered, "I can't believe they wouldn't clear something like this out of here."

"But I don't think—"

"Mitch, trust me on this!" She accidentally kicked an empty bottle, sending it spinning into the street.

"Hey, lady!" Somebody grabbed my mom. She screamed, and smacked the man with her purse as hard as she could.

It was a police officer, in uniform of course.

"What are you, a whacko?" he shouted, rubbing his head.

"Oh my goodness, I'm so sorry," my mom stammered. "I thought you were a purse snatcher. Thank goodness you're here, officer. We got lost, and then we stumbled into this . . . this . . . what are all these homeless people doing here anyway? Isn't this private property . . . oh." She stopped. Her face turned bright red.

I hid my face in my hands.

"Ma'am, you are on a movie lot," the police officer said with exaggerated kindness, as though he were talking to a toddler. "This is a set, and those people are called 'actors.' You know, actors? They are just *pretending* to be homeless. See?" If my mom could sink into the ground, she'd have done it right then. And I'd have jumped in right after her.

"*Cut! Cut!*"

For the first time I noticed a large collection of cameras at the other end of the block. There were enormous lights and a big group of irritated crew people. A man wearing a baseball cap that had the words THE DESPERATE ONE stitched across the brim stomped over to us.

"What's going on here? Why are we having a little tea party in the middle of my shot?"

"This lady got by me before I could stop her. . . ."

"Maybe if you paid more attention to your job instead of that sudoku book, we'd get some work done around here," the director snapped.

The officer's face turned red. Sure enough, he had a sudoku puzzle book in his hand.

"I'm really sorry," my mom mumbled. "We got lost."

The director took a deep breath. "Could you please leave?" he said finally. "We're trying to work here." He turned to the officer. "Would you help this nice lady find her way? *Now?!*"

The officer glared at the director, who glared back. The director's glare won. So the officer led us back around the corner, into the French neighborhood. He showed us where we were on the map and pointed out the bungalow where we were headed. Luckily it wasn't that far from where we were. My mom thanked him, apologized again, and we headed toward the bungalow. She didn't say a word. I knew this was one of those things we'd laugh about in a few months, but right then we were going to pretend it never happened.

When we got to the bungalow there were two people seated outside, a woman and a boy around my age. They watched us uneasily, like a pair of cats watching a couple of bumbling puppies.

"Hello," my mom said. "Is this the audition for Fizzy Whiz Soda?"

"I'm not the receptionist," the woman said, not really answering my mom's question. The woman jerked her thumb at the door.

"Thank you," my mom said, unimpressed by this woman's manners.

We went inside and were finally greeted by a friendly face. It was Hillary, the girl who first brought me into the audition at the recreation center.

"Hi, Mitch!" she gushed as though we were long-lost friends. She turned to my mom. "You must be Mitch's mother. It's so nice to meet you. He's a fabulous kid. You should be very proud."

Both my mom and I wondered what she could possibly be talking about. She had obviously forgotten that I had nearly sent her boss to the emergency room.

I noticed an intense-looking woman seated in a chair next

to a door that led to an inner office. She was trying to hear what was going on in the other room.

"I'm glad you're here—I thought you wouldn't make it," Hillary continued, taking a quick peek at her watch. "I hope you had a chance to look at the sides we sent last night. . . ."

"Sides?" my mom said.

"The script," Hilary said. "'Sides' is what we call the script, or partial script, used in the audition. Do you have any other questions?"

"I do," I piped up. "What's V.O. mean?"

"'Voice-over.' It's when you hear a recorded voice over an image on the screen."

"EXT?"

"That stands for 'exterior.' It means the scene is being shot outside. 'INT' stands for 'interior,' and that it's being shot inside."

"Montage?"

"That's a quick sequence of images or short scenes, one after the other."

"Okay, and how about chyron?"

"It's pronounced 'ky-ron,' and it refers to the words placed over an image. It's done in postproduction, after the commercial has been shot and edited."

"That's it for me," I said.

"Super." Hillary handed me a can of Fizzy Whiz Soda, Razztazztic Raspberry. "Here's a prop you can use to practice," she said. "You'll need it in the audition. Can I get you anything else? Water?"

Water seemed to be everyone's favorite drink in Hollywood. Everywhere we looked there were people guzzling all varieties of water out of bottles. I guess it's because Los Angeles is practically a desert, so Angelenos must get really thirsty. Neither my mom nor I wanted any water. We went back outside.

We sat next to the two unfriendlies. They pretended we weren't there. We all sat in silence for about four minutes, which is a long time to be sitting doing nothing. I started hitting the can against the chair just to fill the silence, but it seemed to annoy the unfriendlies, who moved closer together and whispered to one another.

Finally Hillary opened the door. "Zander Gray?" she said. The boy and his mother rose and went inside. As they did, another boy and the woman who had been seated in the office came out.

"I think I did pretty well," the boy said.

"Did you thank them?"

"Duh, Mom! Of course! And I made one of them laugh."

"Jackpot!" his mom cried, pumping her fist.

Now it was just my mom and me sitting in silence. I started tapping the can again. "Boy, there sure are a lot of golf carts here," I said after a while.

"Mitch, I really don't know about all of this. . . ." my mom began.

"Mom. Please. I know this has been bad so far, but let's just get through it."

She made a sound like a balloon losing air. "All right. Do you want to practice your line?"

"Sure." I composed myself, and then with great enthusiasm I said: "You like babbles?!"

That made her laugh. "C'mon, quit kidding around."

"Okay, okay. I'll try again. You like boobles!? You like bibbles!? Burbles!? How 'bout blubbles?!"

Now my mom was giggling so much she was starting to hiccup. It really wasn't that funny, but I think she just needed to laugh. Suddenly the unfriendlies emerged from the bungalow. My mom tried to stop hiccupping but couldn't. She covered her mouth, but you could still hear snorting, chuckling, and hiccupping from behind her hand. The unfriendlies looked at her as though she was a nut, which only made her laugh harder. They walked away without saying a word, of course.

Hillary poked her head out of the door. "Mitch? Mrs.

Mathis? You can come on in." We followed her inside. She opened the door to the inner office.

"Hee-hee-hee, good luck," my mom hiccupped. "Maybe I will take that water," she added, turning to Hillary.

I took a deep breath and walked through the door.

There were three people in the room, two men and a woman. One man wore jeans, a sweater, and a baseball cap. The other one wore a dark suit. They were seated on a sofa with a coffee table in front of them. On the table was my picture and résumé. The woman was Axel's mom, Mrs. Mulligan. I was sorry to see that she had a big ol' bandage on her forehead, which was barely hiding a purple lump. The man with the baseball cap stood up and smiled warmly.

"Mitch Mathis," he said, extending his hand. I took it and gave it a good shake, which seemed to please him. "Nice to meet you. I'm Alvin Fisher, the director of this commercial, and this is Mr. Baxter from the Fizzy Whiz Company."

"How are you?" the man in the suit said.

"I'm fine, thank you, sir," I said. "And how are you, sir?"

"I'm also well, thank you," he said, amused by my politeness.

"I believe you've already met Mrs. Mulligan," Mr. Fisher said, gesturing to Axel's mom.

"Hello, Mitch," she said pointedly. She was all business. I could tell we were not going to joke about the bandage.

"Hello, Mrs. Mulligan," I answered.

"I understand you are new to this process," Mr. Fisher continued. "Don't be nervous—it's really not hard at all. You are going to be reading with Mrs. Mulligan. Mr. Baxter and I are going to watch. On your cue, which is after Mrs. Mulligan pretends to pour out her flat soda, you ride this unicycle over to her. . . . You do know how to ride a unicycle, right?"

"Yes sir, I'm pretty good," I said.

"Great. So ride the unicycle up to Judy, hop off, say your line, open the soda, and hand her the drink. Are you ready?"

"Is there some specific way you want me to play this Fizzy Whiz character?" I asked.

Mr. Fisher shrugged.

"Surprise us," Mr. Baxter said.

Mrs. Mulligan started reading from the script. Her voice was flat and bored. I could tell she was just trying to get it over with. It dawned on me that Mrs. Mulligan didn't call me back because she wanted to; she did it because she had to. They needed a kid who could ride a unicycle, and I happened to have that skill. The more I thought about it, the more I realized that there was no way in a million years that I could get this part, no matter how well I said the line. After I left the room she would tell them about how I beaned her with a rubber ball. In one second all my confidence drained away. It only took a second, because I didn't have that much confidence to begin with.

Suddenly I realized that Mrs. Mulligan had stopped speaking and was staring at me. She was holding a can of soda upside down as though she had poured out the contents.

That was my cue.

I hopped on the unicycle, rode over to her, and then hopped off. "You like bubbles?" I said, my voice cracking. How embarrassing.

I fumbled with the can and then finally popped it open.

What happened next was not good.

I had forgotten just how much I'd been tapping and shaking that can while I'd been waiting.

A geyser of red soda exploded from the can and hit Mrs. Mulligan square in the eye. It splashed all over her white blouse and her blue sweater. She shrieked and sputtered.

I dropped the can and squeaked an apology, but Mrs. Mulligan didn't care about that. She stomped her foot, sending a spray of soda from her hair around the room.

Then suddenly, as if somebody pressed a button, the director and the Fizzy Whiz executive both leaned back and roared with laughter. They were howling so hard I thought they would die. I really did. Mr. Fisher was curled up on the sofa holding his stomach, groaning.

"That's it!" cried Mr. Baxter, wiping his eyes with his sleeve. "Oh my Lord, we have to add that to the commercial!"

"It's brilliant! 'You like bubbles?' then *Whoosh!* A big squirt right in the kisser!" said Mr. Fisher. "Now *that* is classic comedy!"

"Excuse me, but I am wet," snarled Mrs. Mulligan.

"You should've seen your face, Judy," Mr. Fisher chuckled. "Oh c'mon, lighten up. I'll pay for your dry cleaning. You should be thrilled! We found the Fizzy Whiz Kid!"

"Don't you want to go over all the candidates before you make a decision?"

"I know what I like when I see it," Mr. Baxter said, straightening his suit. "This kid's got the whole package. All-American, messy hair, crooked tooth, freckles . . . that's the face of Fizzy Whiz. And I love the attitude. Everyone loves a rascal, right?"

"Absolutely! Mitch is a natural! He's just like a real-life Huck Finn or Dennis the Menace, sticking his finger in the eye of the stuffy establishment," Mr. Fisher added, clapping a hand on my shoulder.

"Stuffy establishment . . . are you referring to *me?!*" Mrs. Mulligan sputtered.

"Well, yeah! I suppose I am!"

"That's what we're all about," Mr. Baxter added. "That's the Fizzy Whiz attitude! Now sign this kid up, and let's start shooting this thing!"

Mrs. Mulligan left the room to speak with Hillary. Little red footprints dotted the carpet behind her. My mom came in with a confused look on her face. Obviously she had been listening at the door, just like that other mother. I guess once you become a mom nosiness comes with the territory.

"Thank you, Mr. Fisher, Mr. Baxter," I said, remembering my manners.

"No, thank you, Mitch," Mr. Fisher said. "We knew the commercial needed a little more oomph. You gave us just what we needed. And by the way, you can call me Alvin."

My mom was so shocked she'd started hiccupping again. Frankly, I was shocked too. I tried to figure out how I managed to do what I had just done.

THINGS I DID RIGHT IN THE AUDITION

1. I was natural.
2. I was memorable.
3. I had the right look.
4. I made them laugh.

Jackpot.

7
Fizzy Whiz Kid

BY THE TIME I GOT TO SCHOOL, EVERYONE knew I had been at an audition that morning. Kids who I didn't even know came up to me, asking how it went. It felt great to tell them I landed the part. Then they bombarded me with questions: "When's it going to be on?" "How much money are you going to make?" "Do they give you a truckload of free soda?" I had to tell them I didn't know, though I seriously doubted my mom would let me keep a truckload of soda.

"I'm glad you got the part," J.J. said, clipping her hair back with a big ladybug hair clip that matched her ladybug earrings.

"Thanks," I said. "But it was mainly luck."

"Obviously." She plunked herself down in her seat in front of Tangie.

"It's okay," Tangie whispered. "Hollywood runs on luck."

Mrs. Samuelson put a stop to the excitement by handing out a pop quiz.

"Sorry, I squealed," Skywalker admitted later as we headed to the playground for PE. "It was too good a secret to keep to myself."

"Kudos," Dash said as he passed by, punching my arm. "Kudos" means "congratulations." I think it's a word Dash picked up from his dad. "Don't forget us little people on your meteoric rise to the top."

"Yeah, right. And you are . . . ?" I joked.

Just then, Axel and Brandon walked by. Axel didn't look at me, but it was clear that what he was saying was meant for my ears.

"I don't see what the big deal is," he said loudly. "It's not like he's a real actor. He's just holding up a can of soda. A monkey could do that."

"Don't listen to him, he's just jealous," Skywalker muttered.

It didn't bother me that Axel had an attitude. After all, I had wrecked his mother's sweater, not to mention her forehead.

Before we left that day Mrs. Samuelson handed out permission slips for a field trip to the Jet Propulsion Laboratory in Pasadena, which is not far from Los Angeles.

"Make sure you get it back to me. The trip is a month from today," she warned. "No slip, no trip. You'll have to spend the day at home or helping Mrs. Neuman shelve books in the school library."

The class erupted in excited chatter as the bell rang and we gathered up our stuff.

"What's so great about the Jet Propulsion Laboratory?" I asked Skywalker.

"It's a chance to get out of school, that's what."

"It's a lot more than that," Tangie said, overhearing our conversation. "JPL is a NASA center located in CalTech— that's the California Institute of Technology. They made America's first satellite, they just sent a robot up to Mars, and they've got satellites out in space taking pictures of planets . . . and not just the close ones either—the ones that are way, way out there."

"You seem to know an awful lot about it," I said. I was impressed and a little surprised. Tangie didn't fit the description of your typical science nerd.

"That's because *she's* way, way out there," Skywalker joked. Tangie just smiled and shrugged and drifted out the door.

That Thursday was the big day for the commercial shoot. I woke up early enough to see the sun rise. I took a good, long shower where I actually washed my hair. I brushed and flossed and gargled. I dressed in nice clothes with clean socks. Then I went downstairs and ate a breakfast of cereal and juice. I was in such a good mood I cleaned up the kitchen and made my mom and dad a pot of coffee and went outside to get the newspaper. They were both pleasantly surprised. "You should shoot commercials more often," my dad joked.

My mom drove me to the studio, and this time we did not get lost. A young production assistant, Brandy, greeted us at the parking lot. She looked like she was barely out of high school, and she had a really high voice, like a cartoon character. She told us it was her job to help me get ready and introduce me to the crew.

I'm not sure what I expected. I guess I thought shooting the commercial would be like putting on a really short school play where I was the star—and that everyone I met would have big smiles and twinkling eyes just because they felt so lucky and thrilled to be working in show business. Boy, was I way off.

If there's one thing that becomes clear as soon as you start working in show business, it's that it isn't all fun and games. It's a job. You can see it in people's faces. I'm not saying they're miserable (well, some are), but they are definitely at work. People call it the "entertainment industry"—that word, "industry," describes the atmosphere pretty well. It feels like a great big factory where they are putting together a movie or TV show or commercial, and everyone has his job on the assembly line. The weird thing was, I felt like I was the product being assembled.

For instance, our first stop was the costume department, where they took my measurements. The department was in a long, gray building that didn't look like much on the outside. Brandy took me and my mom through a reception area and into a small dressing room, where I was introduced to the costume designer for the commercial. He quickly went about taking my measurements, and he wasn't gentle about it either. He had that tape measure wrapped around me in all kinds of places where I had no idea I was so ticklish, but after I squealed a few times he figured out that maybe he should warn me when he was going to invade my personal space.

After he got my measurements, he started compiling my costume. This involved holding different articles of clothing up to me and muttering personal comments like "He looks terrible in green" and "Those brown jeans make him look like a bum."

"Does he know I'm standing right here?" I murmured to my mom. Green happens to be one of my favorite colors.

"Don't take it personally?" my mom answered in question form. She didn't know what to make of it either, but I could tell she was not impressed by his manners.

The costumer finally settled on a pair of loose denim jeans, a striped blue shirt, and a baggy light-gray trench coat. The inside of the coat had already been fitted with a bunch of elastic loops, each holding a different flavor of Fizzy Whiz Soda: Razztazztic Raspberry, Chocolicious Chocolate, Gulp-It-Down Grape, Crave-It Cotton Candy, Wunderfun Watermelon, and Blowrocious Bubblegum, to name a few. I thought it was going to be hard to move around with all those cans weighing me down, but when I put on the coat I discovered that all the cans were empty.

"Excuse me," I said to the costumer. "But I'm supposed to give the businessman a full can of soda. All these cans are empty."

"Yeah, but people watching the commercial aren't going to know the cans are empty. You get one pre-shaken can right before you need to open it. Don't worry—when it's edited together it'll look right. It's mooovie maaaagic!" He said that last part in a mystical voice and then struggled to keep himself from laughing. Finally he plunked a bright blue cap with the words FIZZY WHIZ stitched on the brim onto my head.

After costumes the next stop on the assembly line was the makeup department. I wasn't crazy about having to wear makeup. The makeup lady explained that everybody who appears on television wears makeup, not just women.

"You know why the news reporter always looks so good, and the person on the street that they're interviewing looks so crummy?" she said as she applied a light tan-colored base to my face. "Makeup! And how about those starlets you see on TV? Like the real gorgeous one on *Kick the Bride*? I've seen that gal without makeup, and let me tell you, it ain't pretty." She added with a shudder, "She's got a face like a cabbage."

It's hard to sit still in a makeup chair. I don't see how models do it. I was there for only twenty minutes, and I wanted to yell, "Stop touching my face!" Then I remembered Mr. Ortega saying he once had to spend hours working on an actor's face to make him look like a pig. Hours! And that actor had to go through that every day! Thank goodness all I needed was a light base makeup, a little red in my cheeks, and darker eyebrows. When I was finished, I thought I looked a little weird, like I'd escaped from a wax museum. The makeup lady said I'd get used to it.

Finally we visited the hair department, which was right next to makeup. This was my shortest stop. After establishing that I'd washed my hair that morning, the hairdresser took off my cap and spun me around in the chair, staring intently at my head. I felt like a cake in a twirling display case. He didn't like something, because he frowned and clucked his tongue.

"Is something wrong?" my mom asked.

"Did anyone ever tell you his head is slightly lopsided?"

That shut my mother up, and me too. I was getting fed up with all these strangers making comments about how I looked. Hey, they didn't look so hot either! I could've really nailed them with some pretty accurate descriptions of my own, but I didn't want to say or do anything that would cause me to lose the job, so I just bit my tongue.

The hairdresser whipped some shears out of a sort of tool belt that he was wearing and started snipping here and snipping there. Then he glopped a lot of mousse in his palm, slapped his hands together, and spread the mixture on my head. He tugged here and he tugged there. Then he delicately placed the cap back on my head and backed away, smiling smugly.

I know this is going to sound vain, but I looked great. I mean really great. Somehow he had taken a hairstyle that looked shaggy but sloppy and turned it into something that looked . . . cool. I could tell my mom approved—or maybe she was just happy I got a free haircut.

"Fantastic!" Brandy said from the door. "Come on, they're waiting for you on the set."

Brandy drove my mom and me to the set in a golf cart. The set was on the "backlot," the same area where my mother and I had gotten lost before the audition. We ended up in the town square with the suburban cottages, but now an outdoor basketball court had been set up in the little park.

Alvin was talking with a cameraman when we arrived. He

waved to my mother as Brandy led her to an area where she could sit, behind the cameras.

"Hi, Mr. Fisher . . . I mean, Alvin," I said. "I'm all ready to go. . . ."

He lowered his sunglasses and looked me over without saying a word. Then he turned the brim of the Fizzy Whiz cap slightly to the side. *"Now* you're ready," he said.

He yelled for the unicycle and the can of soda. The prop master, a man with a bushy mustache, rushed over with the items and handed them to me.

"Okay, Mitch," Alvin said, "I just want to get the shot of you with one hand on the unicycle, like you just hopped off it, and holding the can of soda up to the camera."

"But . . . doesn't that happen at the end of the commercial?" I asked.

"Yes, that's right."

"Well . . . what happened to the rest of it? I didn't even get a chance to try . . ."

Alvin held up his hand. "Whoa, don't worry, we haven't changed the script, but . . . let me see, how can I put this . . ." He thought for a second. "A commercial is like a mini thirty-second movie. Now, movies are just a series of scenes, and a scene is a series of camera shots. You can shoot scenes in any order you want, and the same with camera shots . . . whatever order suits your purposes." He adjusted his cap, just warming up. "For instance, sometimes the order in which you shoot something is determined by the weather or the time of day. Sometimes it depends on the availability of the actor. That's what we have here. I'm shooting as much of your part as I can so that you can go home and not have to hang around here. I'm going to shoot all the basketball stuff last, because we'll probably experiment and shoot a lot of extra footage, so it may take some time. But you don't need to be around for all that, so we're shooting you first. In fact, other than the basketball scene and your scenes, we've already shot the rest of the commercial. It's in the can."

"In the . . . can?" I looked at the soda can, confused.

"No, no, not that can. In the film canister. It's finished. Done. Once I shoot you and the basketball scene, and they're all 'in the can,' I give it to the editor. She puts it in the right order, using the takes that I've told her I like best, or often she'll use her own judgment."

"Wait, what exactly are you taking?" I asked. It was hard to absorb what he was saying, but I really wanted to. This was the kind of technical showbiz information that everybody else in this town seemed to already know, just by living here.

Alvin laughed. "I keep forgetting this is all new to you. A 'take' is what I've shot, from the time the camera starts rolling to the time it stops. It might be an entire scene, or just a few lines. I might have to do several takes of a shot before I'm happy with what I have and move on to the next shot."

"Got it," I said.

"All right. Once the editor has compiled the shots in order, she'll show me what we call a 'rough cut' of the commercial. I'll go back in with her and tinker around with it, sometimes adding things back in, or cutting more away. . . ."

"It sounds like you're sculpting."

"You know, it *is* sort of like sculpting," he said, nodding, "only it's film, not clay. After we get the images and the timing just right, I take it to a postproduction facility, where I lay over the music track that the composer has created and I add sound effects. I direct the voice actor in his voice-over . . . and finally—once I think it's ready—I'll show it to Mr. Baxter, whom you've met. Once he's okay with it, it's ready to air."

"Gee, that's a lot of work for just a thirty-second commercial."

"Yes it is, so we'd better get started." Alvin beckoned to a long-haired, bearded man wearing a headset. "This is Tom, my first assistant director. He's my right-hand man, in charge of making sure everything on the set goes smoothly." Alvin nodded to Tom. "Okay, Tom, we're ready."

Tom carried a clipboard and had an efficient attitude,

like a hall monitor. "Places, everyone!" he called out. People hustled about, getting ready. Alvin took a seat behind the cameraman. He gave me a few directions on where to stand, and when he was satisfied Tom marked the spot with an X made of masking tape.

"That's your mark, Mitch," Tom said. "Stand on it."

"Wait, Al, small problem . . ." It was a woman with short dark hair and rose-colored sunglasses who had also been seated behind the camera.

"Yes, Lucy?"

"The can of soda needs to be open. Supposedly the businessman just got sprayed with it."

"Good point." Alvin popped open the can. "Mitch, this is Lucy, the script supervisor. Lucy's what I like to call the logic police," he said with a wink. "Since we do shoot things out of order, she keeps track of what everything should look like so that it makes sense when it's put together in the editing room." He took a sip from the can of soda and gagged. "Dang, this stuff is sweet!"

"I like it," Lucy said. "So do most of my friends. Maybe it's a generational thing."

"Hey, are you saying I'm old?"

Lucy smirked and went back to her seat.

Alvin made me practice holding up the can a few times,

which was more difficult than you might think. Doing something with fifty people staring at you makes it a hundred times harder. I felt naked; I wanted to run and hide, just get as far away from there as I could. Then I felt a prickly sensation, and suddenly I was hot and sweaty. An instant later I felt cold and shivery. Then suddenly I couldn't breathe. That was a horrible feeling. If I fainted, I'd lose the part for sure. But I didn't faint, and the more we practiced, the more I was able to relax and concentrate on what I had to do.

I had to make sure the label was visible and straight. I had to have a certain expression on my face, which took a while to find, and then I had to remember that expression and repeat it several times. And I had to stay on my mark. Alvin did three takes. Each take was marked by a "clapboard," a square chalkboard with the name of the shot on it (this shot was called "FWK holding can"), and a number indicating which take it was. That was how Alvin marked the shots for the editor to identify later in the editing room. The chalkboard had a movable hinged top that you could clap down with a loud *smack*. Later Alvin explained that the smack sound was necessary to sync up the film track with the sound track. It wasn't like videotaping something on your home video camera; it was a lot more complicated!

After he shot me holding up the can, Alvin directed me to

ride the unicycle through the basketball players and up to the businessman. The actor playing the businessman had a bald, egg-shaped head and a long, pointy nose. I actually recognized him from a copy-machine billboard that I'd seen years ago. His face was that memorable.

"I'm sorry I'm going to have to squirt you with the soda, sir," I said.

"Hey, I'm not a knight, you don't have to call me 'sir,'" he said with a laugh. "We're working together. Call me Edward. And don't worry about the soda. I've been hit with a lot worse: cream pies, mud, paint . . . I once had to dive into a swimming pool filled with spaghetti and meatballs. That's what I get paid for. Besides, I've got a great reaction."

Edward puffed up his cheeks and bugged out his eyes. He looked like a blowfish about to throw up. It was the craziest-looking face I've ever seen, and believe me, I've spent a lot of time—more time than I'd care to admit—in front of a mirror coming up with crazy-looking faces. Edward's face blew all my faces out of the water.

But Edward wasn't finished. He blinked a few times, twitched his nose, and then with a snarl he mimed grabbing the can and taking a big gulp of soda. His whole body seemed to wriggle, and then his eyes lit up like a pinball machine. I cracked up.

"See?" Edward said. "But don't laugh while I'm doing it, or we'll never get home tonight."

He shouldn't have said that. It totally jinxed me. We had to do *sixteen* takes of me squirting him with the soda before we got one where I wasn't cracking up. To be fair, Edward was trying to make me laugh. It was obvious.

As we drove home, I suddenly felt exhausted. I had trouble keeping my eyes open, even though the sun was still up. My mom told me she was very proud of me. I had forgotten she had been sitting back there, watching the whole thing, but now she told me how it looked from her perspective. She thought it all went well, and she liked the director a lot. She thought Edward was a big ham. She thought Lucy shouldn't wear such a tight shirt. She was smiling, but I detected a weird sadness in her voice. I didn't know why until that night.

I was about to go into my parents' bedroom to say good night when I overheard them whispering, which meant they didn't want me to know what they were saying. So of course I placed my ear to the door so that I could hear better.

"He was really good," my mom was saying.

"That's great!" my dad said, but my mom must've had a look on her face, because then he said, "Yes? No? What's the matter?"

"Grant, Mitch didn't look over at me once. Not once during the entire shoot."

"Well, honey, it was awfully exciting for him. . . ."

"I know, I know. I'm not saying he did anything wrong, but . . . I guess it suddenly hit me that, well . . . he didn't need me."

"Mitch needs you. He just didn't look at you. He knew you were there, though."

"I don't know. This show-business kick is his thing. He chose it, he's going with it, and today he was fearless. I was the one with butterflies in my stomach. But Mitch looked like he was right at home. I guess . . . he's growing up. He's starting to slip away."

"Hmm. Well, maybe so," my dad said. There was a pause. I guessed he had put an arm around my mom and was holding her close. They do that when I'm not around . . . or when they think I'm not around.

"Good for him," my dad said gently. "Good for him."

They were probably going to start kissing, so I went back to my room. I crawled into bed, and even though I was exhausted, it took me a while to fall asleep. What a weird day it had been. It started out kind of scary, and then while I was "on the assembly line" it became irritating, but now, looking back, I think it was the best day of my life.

8

Celebrity

THE NEXT FEW WEEKS ZOOMED BY. I WAS so excited about the commercial that I could barely concentrate on homework, but I'd promised my dad I wouldn't let my grades drop, so I forced myself to muscle through it.

The one thing that did take my mind off the commercial was helping the Ortegas decorate their house for Halloween. By the time we were finished there were ghouls hanging out the windows, hundreds of spiders crawling up the walls, and a cemetery with zombies clawing their way out of the ground. Best of all, Mr. Ortega rigged a projector into the branches of the tree in their front yard. When you turned it on, it projected ghostly figures zooming across the front of the house.

Finally the big night came: not Halloween, but the premiere of the Fizzy Whiz commercial. It was scheduled to air during the World Series, which J.J. told me is supposed to be an excellent time to air a commercial because so many people are glued to the TV set. I invited Skywalker and Dash over. We ordered a pizza and salad and bought some ice-cream bars, and Skywalker brought some chips, while Dash showed up with mixed nuts and a plant, which he said was a housewarming gift from his parents. My mom and dad had gone out and bought a big TV. It wasn't nearly as big as Skywalker's theater screen, but it was big enough.

The baseball game started. I love baseball, but I barely even remember which teams were playing; I only cared about the commercial. In fact, we took our bathroom breaks during the game so that we wouldn't miss one second of the commercials.

Then, after the top of the fifth inning, the Fizzy Whiz commercial aired! It went by so fast I wasn't sure what I'd seen. I just remember watching myself on the unicycle, flapping around in that weird coat, Edward's face splashed with soda, his hilarious reaction, and then my big head filling up the screen until I pushed the can in front of it. In the next instant the game was back on.

"Aw, man, now *that* was *funny!*" Skywalker howled, pounding me on the back.

"Excellent, Mitch!" Dash laughed. "Where'd they find that crazy-looking coat?"

"I thought that went pretty well," my dad said, sounding a little surprised. "Didn't you, dear?"

"I thought that cap looked a little sloppy," my mom said.

"That was on purpose, Mom. Alvin wanted it that way."

"You mean Mr. Fisher?" she said pointedly. She didn't much care for my calling an adult by his first name.

"Well, this is all very, very good," my dad said. "I'm glad this little adventure turned out well. As I always say, it never hurts to try something new. No amount of book learning beats firsthand experience. I remember the first time I actually heard a hissing cockroach in person. . . ." He started talking about something that the rest of us didn't care about.

But the adventure was far from over.

It was just the beginning.

The next day at school, everyone who saw the commercial congratulated me. They all liked the soda spurting in Edward's face the best, and to tell the truth, they gave me a lot more credit than I probably deserved. It was Edward's reaction that was funny; all I said was "You like bubbles?" but somehow that little question became a big thing. All day kids came up to me shouting, "Hey! You like bubbles?" and then cracking up.

In class Tangie winked at me and gave me the "A-OK" sign as I sat down. She passed me a note that said, "Cute commercial! You're naturally funny!" I changed her note so that it said, "naturally funny looking," and passed it back. She smiled and then wrote something and passed the note back. She'd drawn a happy face with freckles and a snaggletooth, and a voice balloon saying "You like bubbles?"

Most of the rest of the kids in class had also seen it, and told me they liked it. J.J. for some reason wanted to give me some "notes."

"You need to be a little more sly, a little more, you know, like you're playing a prank," she said. "It's not clear whether or not you're hitting him with the soda on purpose. And when you smile, wrinkle your nose. It shows off that tooth."

"Why are you telling me this? The commercial is finished," I said.

"For next time," she said. "Believe me, there will be a next time."

I have to say, all of the attention did make me feel pretty popular. But then it went to a whole new level.

After school I had a dentist appointment. My mom drove me to the medical building, and when we got out of the car, the parking attendant gave me a strange look. As my mom and I headed to the elevator I noticed him talking with the other parking attendant and pointing at me.

The elevator was full, but we scrunched ourselves in

anyway. I got banged in the ear by a woman's purse as she pushed the button to her floor.

"I'm sorry," she said.

"That's okay."

She gave me a strange look. "Are you . . . are you the boy in the commercial? The one with the soda?"

"Yes, that was me," I said.

"I knew it!" Suddenly she was very excited. "You look just like yourself!"

My mom gave her a stiff smile and smoothed down my hair, but the woman kept going, turning to the man behind her.

"You know that commercial during the baseball game? The one with the soda? This is the kid!"

"Ohhh," the man said, craning his neck to see. "That was really funny. I love that commercial!"

"Thank you," I said. The elevator door opened and some more people got in. Their eyes widened with recognition, but in the next second my mom had already hustled me out.

"Wait, Mom, this isn't our floor. . . ."

"Oh, it isn't? Well, we'll just have to use the stairs. I don't want to wait for the next elevator." She totally knew it wasn't our floor.

Three people in the waiting room had seen the commercial. The receptionist had seen the commercial. The dentist and his assistant had seen the commercial. A little kid asked for my autograph, but he didn't have a piece of paper, so I signed his hand. He ran over and showed his mom, and she gave me a huge smile, like I'd saved his life.

"Thank you!" she gushed. It seemed a little much.

On the way home my mom had a concerned look on her face. "Mitch, I want you to be careful. I don't like all those strangers coming up and talking to you."

"Mom, I'm not a baby."

"I know, but Los Angeles is a big city. Just keep your guard up."

The next day at school was more of the same. Some people who hadn't seen the commercial during the game had seen it since then, and they came up and congratulated me. I was becoming the most recognized kid in school. The only bad thing that happened was that at lunchtime a few kids had brought soda with them and started squirting each other with it. That brought out the vice principal, who I found out was also the dean of discipline. That afternoon he announced over the PA system that soda was no longer allowed in lunches; from now on only water, milk, juice, and other noncarbonated beverages were acceptable.

After school I was about to walk home with Dash and Skywalker when someone called out, "Hey, Mitch, hold up!" I turned around. It was Brandon.

"I saw your commercial. Hilarious," he said. "Was it fun to shoot?"

"Yeah, it was pretty fun," I said. I was about to turn around, but to my surprise he kept on talking.

"That guy who played the businessman, I've seen him in some other things. He's really talented. I'm surprised he doesn't have his own TV show."

"His name's Edward. He was a nice guy," I said. "He told me he used to be a stand-up comedian but got tired of having to perform for a bunch of drunks at two o'clock in the morning."

Brandon laughed, more than he needed to. Then he got to the point. "Listen, I'm having a little birthday party a week from Saturday. Why don't you come over? Bring your whole family." He handed me an invitation with my name written on the envelope in beautiful calligraphy.

"Wow! Really?!" I couldn't hide my enthusiasm. I'd heard that Brandon lived in a huge mansion. I'd never been inside a mansion before, except for a tour of the White House, in Washington, D.C.

"Sure," Brandon said. "I hope you can make it."

He turned and jogged back to J.J. and Axel, who glowered at me with his hands thrust in his pockets. I put the invitation in a separate pocket of my backpack. I didn't want to lose it. I didn't even want to ding the corners of the envelope; they were so perfectly straight. You could slice cheese with that envelope.

"Finished talking to your new best friend?" Dash teased, but there was an edge in his voice. I knew right away that he hadn't been invited to the party.

"So are you guys going to come over for Halloween to hand out candy?" Skywalker said, changing the subject.

"I've got to take my sister around with her friends," Dash said. "But we'll try to come by."

"I'll be there," I said. "But I don't want to be anywhere near the cemetery. It already creeps me out."

"All right. I'll man the cemetery. You just hand candy out at the door. Can you handle that?"

"Oh, no doubt. Mitch can handle anything. Mitch is a multitalented sensation." Dash hitched his backpack onto his shoulders. "I've got to stop by the 7-Eleven. See you." He didn't ask if we wanted to join him.

"Don't mind him," Skywalker said after Dash was gone. "He's just mad about you being invited to Brandon's party. He wasn't."

"That's what I figured," I said. "You know, at my old school you had to either invite everyone in the class or just have a small party, like two or three people."

"They have the same rule here. You just happen to be one of Brandon's two or three people, my friend." Skywalker said with a grin.

"But I barely know Brandon."

"You're on his radar. Enjoy it while it lasts."

"I don't know what's bugging Dash, then. If most of the kids weren't invited, why did he expect to be?"

"Dash doesn't want to go to the party!" Skywalker laughed. "He hates Brandon. Brandon's dad is a studio executive, and he fired Dash's dad off a hundred-million-dollar movie project after Dash's dad had written two drafts of the script. Goldwyn called him an intellectual snob who couldn't write a joke to save his grandmother. Then Dash's dad said that he didn't need writing tips from a Neanderthal who thought every joke should end with a fart. Brutal, right? But he paid for it. Dash's dad couldn't get work after that."

"Ouch."

"You're telling me. Anyway, it started a feud between Dash and Brandon. Dash always reminds Brandon that he is way smarter than him, and Brandon always gets back at him somehow. Like, remember when I told you Dash and I had tried to start a band? Well, last year Brandon discovered a bunch of lyrics Dash wrote, but they weren't quite ready. They sounded like corny love poems, and Brandon sent them out to all the girls in the class, signing Dash's name. It was pretty embarrassing. That was the end of the band."

"Well, if it's going to make Dash mad, maybe I shouldn't go."

"Are you nuts? Go! Have fun! I've been to Brandon's place—it's awesome. I'll handle Dash. He gets a little prickly sometimes, but he always comes around."

The next day was Halloween. Everyone was supposed to come to school in a costume. I went as a bank robber. I wore a black ski mask, black turtleneck, jeans, and my mom's black gloves and carried a bright green water pistol. I was way underdressed! Most of the costumes kids wore looked like professional works of art. It was obvious their parents had either put a lot of time and effort into creating these outfits or had paid gobs of money. One kid, whose mom designed costumes for the Los Angeles Opera, came as a Chinese emperor. Tangie wore a 1920s flapper outfit that her mom had worn in a gangster movie. Skywalker's goblin costume came straight from his dad's workshop. Dash's costume was brilliant: He came as a bulletin board, with funny notes attached to himself. Brandon wore a real silk top hat and carried an ivory-handled cane. He was the millionaire from the Monopoly board game. J.J. came as a spider, and she wore glasses with eight lenses, for each of her eight eyes. Axel was a vampire, wearing a real tuxedo, a lot of jewelry, red contact lenses, and incredibly realistic vampire teeth. It was the perfect costume for him.

Mrs. Samuelson, dressed as the Queen of Hearts, reminded us again to bring in our permission slips for the Jet Propulsion Laboratory. After that there was a parade of the entire school and a carnival fundraiser. We didn't do any schoolwork at all. I would never think of Halloween as being just kid stuff anymore. In Hollywood, Halloween was as big as Christmas.

I went over to Skywalker's place around dusk. We ate pizza, and then he led me to the bucket of candy I'd be manning. It was not really a bucket; it was a cauldron with green slime on the sides, filled to the brim with chocolate bars.

"What, did you buy out the whole store?" I said. "How many kids are you expecting?"

"Hundreds. Maybe even a thousand."

"A thousand! You've got to be kidding!"

"Our house is very popular," Skywalker said proudly. "And we're not the only ones in this neighborhood who decorate our house this much, you know. There's a set designer down the block who competes with my dad to design the scariest haunted house, and last year a pair of costume designers moved in around the corner. They had a whole Victorian theme going on. It was pretty awesome!"

At sunset Skywalker's dad turned on all the equipment: the projector, the sound machine, the fog maker, and the strobe lights. About a minute later the doorbell rang. I heard a scream, which meant Skywalker had just jumped out from behind a tombstone in his goblin getup. That was my signal. I opened the door. Trick-or-treating had begun.

It was the first time I had handed out candy instead of trick-or-treating myself, and it was actually kind of fun. Little kids are always the first ones around, in their cute costumes. The girls are all princesses, and the boys are all superheroes or firemen, and they barely even know what to say. They usually have their parents behind them, reminding them to say "trick or treat" and "thank you," and reminding them to take only one piece of candy. It's no wonder the kids are confused; all year their parents warn them not to take candy from strangers, and then all of a sudden they tell them to do just that.

After the little kids finished, the older kids made their rounds, without parents. These are the kids who either want to gross you out or make you laugh. There were a lot of ax murderers, a patient with guts spilling out, a kid dressed like a banana, another dressed like a cell phone, a group of go-go girls, and a handful of hippies. Then came the strangest costume of all.

A kid rolled up to the porch on a unicycle. He wore a

messy wig, fake buck teeth, freckles, big rubber ears, and a huge overcoat. He hopped off the unicycle and shoved his bag at me. "Trick or treat!" he shouted. "You like bubbles?"

I couldn't believe it.

He jammed his hand into the cauldron, pulled out a fistful of candy, and then said, "My costume's a lot better than yours. Where's your big coat?"

As he rolled away, Skywalker joined me on the steps, pulling off his goblin mask.

"Wow, that was weird," he said.

"Do I really look like that?"

"Um . . . well, yeah, you do," he said. Then he laughed. "You've hit the big time, Mitch! You, my friend, are a costume!"

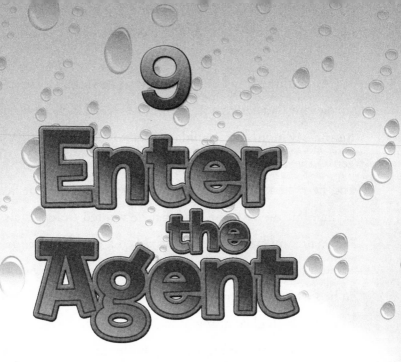

9
Enter the Agent

THE NEXT DAY I GOT A CALL FROM J.J.'S dad, Jeremy Schwartz.

He phoned during dinner, so we let the answering machine get it. His voice was so loud it sounded like he was right there in the room with us.

"Hello? Hello? This is Jeremy Schwartz of Creative Quest Agency. My daughter J.J. tells me there's a brand-new TV star in her class, a young Mr. Mitchell Mathis. Mitch, I took a look at your work—it's outstanding. I want you to give me a call right away. Call me at home."

He then left his phone number, again urging me to call him immediately.

After dinner my father called Mr. Schwartz. His voice was so loud my dad had to hold the phone several inches away from his ear. My mom and I could hear the whole conversation from across the room. Mr. Schwartz talked a lot. He talked loud, and he talked fast. It was hard to keep up with what he was saying, but the gist of it was that he wanted to represent me. Normally my father would have asked a lot of questions, but I could tell he was getting tired of listening to Mr. Schwartz, so he finally agreed to meet with him tomorrow. As soon as he hung up, he looked at my mom and rolled his eyes.

"I don't want to meet this guy," he said. My mom, who, as I said before, loves my dad more than anything, said she'd do it, even though I could tell she wasn't crazy about meeting Jeremy Schwartz either. But the date was set. We would meet him tomorrow at the office in Beverly Hills at four o'clock.

The next day J.J. grabbed me before class started. "I hear you're seeing my dad today. I really talked you up, so don't blow it."

"Thanks, I guess," I said.

"You guess? You *guess?* Good grief, Mitch, most people would be thrilled if they got a call from Jeremy Schwartz . . . *the* Jeremy Schwartz! My dad's the top talent agent in town. He's taken people with less talent than you and turned them into very wealthy people. *Very, very* wealthy. There isn't one executive—not one!—who wouldn't drop everything to take a phone call from him. When Jeremy Schwartz calls, the industry sits up and pays attention. And I'm not just saying that because I'm his daughter. It's the truth."

J.J. clearly had a very high opinion of her father, which was understandable. What I didn't understand was why she had such a high opinion of me, but who was I to argue? "What should I expect?" I asked.

"Expect to be blown away," she said with a smirk. And she plunked herself down in her seat. Then she pounded Tangie's desk to startle her out of her daydream, just because she was in such a good mood. Dash, who had warmed up a bit from the other day, passed me on his way to his desk.

"Don't believe her. Her dad's just a big, loud jerk," he whispered.

"Why is she helping me?" I said.

"I think she likes you," Skywalker said with a snicker. So of course I punched him.

Creative Quest Agency is in the swankiest area of downtown Beverly Hills, near Rodeo Drive, where all the stars go shopping. When we drove into the parking garage, a valet was waiting to take my mom's car. The valet was wearing a very spiffy-looking dark blue uniform with a military-looking cap with a shiny black brim and a gold cord across the top. My mom dropped her keys trying to hand them to him and then bumped heads with him when they both tried to pick them up. Nerves.

We approached the guard sitting in the center of a doughnut-shaped desk in an entry that could've doubled as a museum hall. No kidding—if for some reason the Natural History Museum needed a place to store its dinosaur displays, it could easily fit them all right here. And you could throw in a couple of killer whales from SeaWorld to keep them company.

"Helen Mathis and Mitchell Mathis," my mom said. "We have an appointment with Jeremy Schwartz."

"One moment please." The guard called Mr. Schwartz's office and then asked us to sign the registry. After he gave us a couple of official-looking guest passes to wear on our shirts, he walked us over to the bank of elevators. He pressed the button for us, and when we got inside he swiped a card over a light and pressed the button to the top floor. The doors swished closed, and we enjoyed the smoothest elevator ride I'd ever experienced. I could hardly tell the darn thing was even moving.

My mom and I were both very impressed.

The receptionist on the top floor told us that Mr. Schwartz's assistant would be with us shortly. We sat on the white leather couch, which made embarrassing squeaky noises whenever you shifted your butt. After five minutes of me squeaking around and my mom giving me dirty looks, a young woman with dark hair and glasses appeared around the corner. She zipped across the reception area like a speed walker, her heels click-clacking on the floor.

"Hi, I'm Amy, Jeremy's assistant. He's on a conference call to France right now, but he wanted me to see if there was anything I can get you. Would you like a bottle of water?"

No, we didn't. Amy disappeared as fast as she had come.

Thirty minutes later she came back. This time she led us through a maze of modern-looking cubicles with young people at computers, talking on headsets. They all spoke very quickly and sounded very important. I felt like I was in the Pentagon.

Amy showed us into a corner office. The first thing I noticed was that two of the walls were floor-to-ceiling windows, and through them you could see the famous Hollywood sign, stretching across the hills, directly in line with Mr. Schwartz's desk. He was pacing around the room, yelling into his headset. He gestured for us to take a seat on the sofa. Instead of the squeaky white leather, his sofa had big, soft, velvet cushions. When my mom and I sat down we sank so low it felt as if we were disappearing into quicksand.

Mr. Schwartz took off the headset. "Amy, hold my calls!" he shouted. He shut the door and started talking.

"You must be Mrs. Marshall. It's a pleasure to meet you," he said, extending his hand.

"Actually, it's Mrs. Mathis," my mom corrected, but Mr. Schwartz wasn't listening.

"What's your first name, dear?"

"Helen . . ."

"Helen. Perfect. It suits you. Helen. May I call you Helen? Call me Jeremy. We really should be on a first-name basis, Helen, because we are going to get to know each other really well."

My mom looked slightly shocked, as though she had been locked in the room with a lunatic. "How do you figure, Mr. Schwartz?"

"Mr. Schwartz is my father. Call me Jeremy. Please. What I mean is, I've been following your son's work, and it is nothing short of extraordinary. I want to be in business with him. I want to be in the Mitch Marshall business."

"It's Mathis, and he's only done the one commercial."

"And what he was able to do with those three little words is nothing short of genius. 'You like bubbles?' Hahahahah! It was like . . . poetry. Short, funny poetry. Hilarious haiku. Beautiful. You don't see talent like this every day, at least I don't, and it's my business to look for it. What we have here is a diamond, Helen, a diamond in the rough. You may not see it, but Mitch here has *it.*"

"*It?*"

"Exactly. Some people have it, some people don't. It's not something you can learn or mimic or buy, it's that *thing*, Helen, that *it* thing that people—the public—love. Savvy?"

My mom opened her mouth to say something, but Jeremy wasn't finished.

"I know what you're going to say. You're going to say, 'Jeremy, this is all moving too fast. Mitch is just a regular kid with a regular life. We're not sure this is the direction we want to go with him, this is all very confusing, we need to think about it for a while.'"

My mom nodded. "Yes, something like . . ."

"Ah! But there's a problem with that, Helen. In show business you've got to move fast. You can't think. If you think, you're dead in the water."

"That explains a lot," my mom muttered.

"You've got to strike while the iron's hot. People want to see more of Mitch, and they want to see it *now*, not in a month or a year. When you're hot, you're hot. Right now he's a three-alarm fire."

"But he's only done one little comm—"

"What do you think about all this, Mitch?" Jeremy

interrupted, turning to me. "Are you uncomfortable with all this? Too shy to be in the limelight? Just a regular kid who wants to lead a regular life? Or do you want to go for it?" When he said "go for it," I could've sworn his eyes sparkled. What can I say? A talent agent is a salesman, and he sold me. Who would want to live a regular life when you could have the sparkle? Suddenly I realized this was bigger than just fitting in at school. For the first time in my life, I had a chance to be special, to be the person everyone else envied. Me, Mitch Mathis, king of the hill. And Jeremy was right: It was now or never.

I looked at my mom with big puppy-dog eyes. "Mom . . . ?"

"I don't know, Mitch. . . ."

"I'll keep my grades up. . . ."

She sat silently, mulling it over. Both Jeremy and I knew this was a critical moment. He gave me a look, and I could tell he was telling me to sit tight, that he would handle it. But he didn't know my mom the way I know my mom. If he tried to bluff or strong-arm her, if she sensed he was underestimating her intelligence in any way, we would be on the elevator taking a smooth ride to the parking garage, and that would be the end of it. I gave him a look that tried to express all of that. A slight movement in his eyelid let me know that he understood.

Jeremy took a deep breath. Incredibly, his voice got

softer. "Look, Mrs. Mathis. I can see that you are not the sort of person who is sucked in by the glitz and glamour of Hollywood. I admire you for that. All of us here sometimes get caught up in the excitement of this industry and forget that there are more important things going on in the world. When it comes right down to it, selling soda is really not all that important. I probably seem very shallow to you and maybe even a little pathetic, the way I go on and on about that silly commercial—but I have to admit, I do love show business. Every little part of it. It's the kind of industry where every single person, from the director to the kid who runs out and gets people sandwiches at lunchtime, is important.

"You know, folks sometimes call this place a dream factory, and it is. But the way I see it, dreams aren't just useless, fluffy things floating around in people's heads—dreams *are important*. Every meaningful event or invention or social movement started as a dream. Now I grant you that movies and television can sometimes be dumb. In fact, some are barely watchable. But here's what else they can be: a welcome respite after a tough day at work. A mirror showing us our strengths and weaknesses. They can be a guide showing us how to handle tough situations. They can be a unifying force, drawing millions into a single shared experience that will be talked about in the days, months, and years to come. They can be a vessel transporting you to see people and places you've never dreamed of seeing. They can be a time machine to the past and the future. And, every once in a while, they can be a seed. The seed of a new idea . . . an idea that, planted in the right person, can blossom into something profound.

"So you see, entertainment isn't just a money-making machine, though it is that too, I won't lie to you. Mitch has a chance to be part of it. He's lucky. He may not get this chance again. A lot of kids who get this chance have parents with your very same concerns, and I'll tell you something: As long as *you* keep *your* head level, Mitch will too. Who knows? Maybe he'll really be something big, but even if he isn't, he'll have made enough money to pay for a college education at the school of his choice.

"So that's my pitch. Go home, talk about it with your husband, listen to Mitch. He seems mature enough to take some responsibility for his life. Then give me a call, let me know one way or the other. And thanks for coming down here to listen to me. I do like to hear myself talk."

Jeremy helped my mom un-wedge herself from the couch and then lifted me out as well. He led us to his door, opened it, and shook both of our hands again.

"It was very nice to meet you." He turned to Amy, who was seated in a cubicle close to his office. "Amy, please see the

Mathises to the elevator and validate their parking. Give them an extra hour in case they want to walk around a little."

We took a smooth elevator ride back to the lobby. Since we had an extra hour, we walked to a coffee shop. My mom got a cappuccino, and I got a fancy hot chocolate with whipped cream and chocolate sprinkles.

"He sure can talk," my mom said. I smiled.

Jeremy had done it.

I actually suspected he had a slam dunk when we were still wedged in his sofa and he started his speech. That was why he was so good at his job. He can read people, the same way I can. He knew how to handle my mom as soon as we walked in the room. And you know what? Looking back on it, I think that all of his annoying jibber-jabber at the beginning of the meeting was just to set her up for the speech at the end, a speech that he's probably made over and over again, no matter how "spur of the moment" he made it look. Watching him talk had been like watching a magician. And even though my mom probably knew his sincerity was a little rehearsed, she fell for it anyway, because, just like with magic, deep down she wanted to believe him. All she needed was an excuse.

We talked it over with Dad, but he could see Mom's mind was made up, and because he loves her as much as she loves him, he didn't put up much of a fuss. My dad's motto is "Let's give it a shot," and that's exactly what he said after she told him how the meeting went.

She called Jeremy. Again we could hear his voice through the receiver from across the room.

"Hello, Mr. Schwartz, I hope I'm not interrupting your dinner. . . ."

"Not at all. I'm still at the office, Mrs. Mathis. What can I do for you? Have you come to a decision?"

"Yes, I think we will give it a shot."

"Oh, that is wonderful news, Mrs. Mathis. I am very, very happy to hear that. I'm going to get the Fizzy Whiz people on the phone right now and let them know."

"Let them know what?"

"Well, while I was waiting, I poked around to see if they were going to make another commercial, since the first one is so popular. It turns out they are planning a series of commercials. They want Mitch in all of them."

"What?! When did all this happen?"

"That was their plan right from the beginning, Helen. They just wanted to wait to see how the first commercial went. But you see, that's where I come in. They were prepared to offer Mitch a rock-bottom, lowball offer for the next five commercials. But that's not right. Mitch *is* the Fizzy Whiz Kid. They can make a commercial without Christopher Columbus, they can make it without the sad mom and her saggy soufflé, they can make it without the hip, happenin' basketball dudes. They *can't* make it without Mitch. Mitch has what you call 'leverage,' and I'm going to use it. I'll get back to you soon."

My mom hung up, stunned. "I think he knew I was going to call," she said.

Two hours later, at nine o'clock, Jeremy called back. He was still at the office. He had some good news. I would get five more commercials, guaranteed, which meant that if they didn't use me in them, they would have to pay me anyway. Additionally I would get my own dressing room, my own parking space, and much more money than what I got paid for the first commercial. My mom has always told me that it's poor manners to talk about how much money you make, so I'll just put it this way: I will definitely be able to pay for the college of my choice and have enough left over for a pretty sweet car!

10
Arabian Nights

ON SATURDAY MY PARENTS AND I GOT dressed up to go to Brandon's birthday party. My mom insisted we wear nice clothes because of the quality of the paper used for the invitation. When I first showed it to her, she was really impressed by the thick, creamy envelope and the fact that the lettering was engraved.

"This is nicer than my wedding invitations," she had said.

The invitation had a golden Arabian lamp at the top and scimitars at each corner. The words, also in gold, read:

Open Sesame!
You and your family are invited to
an Evening of Wonders

To celebrate
Brandon Goldwyn's 13th Birthday
Saturday, November 10
4:00 P.M.
161223 Mulholland Drive
RSVP 323-555-8181

My mom also insisted on picking up a bouquet of flowers at the grocery store for Brandon's parents. "When invited to a party, you must always give the hostess something. It is just good manners," she had said.

It took me a while to pick out a gift for Brandon because I had no idea what he liked. The only thing I could think of was a mirror, but I wasn't going to get him that. I ended up buying him a gift certificate to an online music store.

"I'm still not sure I understand why we're all invited," my father said as we drove up into the Hollywood Hills. "I haven't stayed with you at a birthday party since you were in kindergarten."

"I guess Brandon's parents want to meet you," I said, though I couldn't think of one reason why they would.

The houses in the Hollywood Hills ranged from rickety cottages built on stilts and barely hanging on to the side of the hill, to fancy mansions filling up every inch of their lots.

As we climbed higher and higher into the hills, it got harder and harder to see the houses; as huge as they were, most of them still managed to hide behind even huger hedges or walls.

Suddenly we found ourselves behind a long line of cars. "I wonder if there's been an accident up there," my dad said, craning his head out the window.

It wasn't an accident. It was valet parking. We finally pulled up to the five young guys wearing crisp, white shirts, black vests, and black pants. They were rushing back and forth, helping people out of their cars, handing them tickets, and then driving the cars away. One of them tapped on my mom's door, and she unlocked it. The valet offered her his hand.

"Good evening, ma'am. How are you today?"

"I'm fine, thanks," my mom said, laughing nervously. I guess to her his outfit looked like a uniform. "And, ah, ha ha, how about yourself?" she said. I cringed. She was actually trying to impress the valet with her good manners.

"Very well, thank you." He helped her out and opened the door for me.

"Hello, young man, just follow the sword jugglers into the party."

"Sword jugglers?"

He winked. "You'll see."

By that time another valet had given my dad a ticket, climbed into our car, and zoomed off.

I turned to take a look at the house. Well, actually I wasn't looking at the house; I was looking at a gigantic wall with a bunch of security cameras on top of it. The top was also lined with pointy spears, I guess to discourage anyone who didn't notice the cameras.

We followed the people ahead of us through an iron gate where we were met by bare-chested sword jugglers standing across from each other, creating a path to the backyard. They whipped scimitars around their bodies and then flipped them into the air and caught them again. It did not look easy. I wondered what might have happened if I had been juggling scimitars instead of rubber balls at the talent search. Mrs. Mulligan wouldn't have a head, that's what.

My parents were uneasy about the jugglers, so we made a wide detour around the "path of death."

Past the sword jugglers stood the mansion. It had a kind of Spanish-Mediterranean design and looked like a pink palace. The house was three stories surrounded by palm trees and bushes with gigantic flowers. A sweet smell filled the air.

We could hear music: flutes, horns, drums, and a sitar,

which is kind of like a high-pitched guitar with a long, skinny neck. We followed the sounds into the backyard. Here's what we found there:

THE BACKYARD OF WONDERS

1. Five huge striped tents
2. A catered Mediterranean feast that did not include pizza or hot dogs
3. A kids' feast that did include pizza and hot dogs
4. A dessert feast that included an ice-cream-sundae bar
5. A real bar with wine, beer, soft drinks, tea, fancy coffee, milk, and juice
6. Musicians surrounded by huge pillows where people could sit, eat, and talk
7. Strolling belly dancers
8. Three camels, used for camel rides
9. Sand sculptures of an elephant, a camel, a hippo, and Brandon
10. Hundreds of lit torches
11. A lagoon-type pool with candles floating in it
12. A belly dancer with a live tiger on a leash and another with an orangutan on her shoulders

"Who is this party for, the kids or the parents?" my dad gasped as one of the belly dancers wiggled by.

My mom just stared out at the view of Los Angeles, which was tremendous. We were at the tip-top of the Hollywood Hills, looking over the rest of Los Angeles, which in midafternoon had a thick haze of smog over everything. We were looking down on it, though. Brandon lived above the smog.

An older woman approached us. She was draped in silk, which I guess was supposed to be some kind of Arabian outfit. She was also wearing a painfully tight smile, and it looked like she couldn't remove it even if she wanted to.

"Hello!" she said. "I'm Lorna Goldwyn. And you are . . . ?"

"We're the Mathis family," my dad said. "This is Helen, and I'm Grant. It's very nice to meet you, Lorna."

My mom was still clutching the invitation, proof that we hadn't snuck in uninvited. She held out the little grocery-store bouquet.

"Thank you for inviting us to your home," my mom said.

"Oh, you shouldn't have," Lorna said, taking the flowers. I looked at the sad little daises and carnations, which had wilted from the heat of my mom's hand. Mrs. Goldwyn was right; we really shouldn't have. She turned to me. "You must be Mitch, from Brandon's class."

"Yes, ma'am," I said. "Do you know where I can find him?"

"Oh, he's inside the house somewhere," she said. "Just go through the back door. Someone can direct you."

"Thank you." I turned to my mom and dad, who looked like a couple of lost kids. "I'll see you later," I said. I dashed up the hill to the back door of the house.

Everything I'd heard about Brandon's home was true. It was huge. To look at it you would think a family of giants lived there. Everything in the house was supersized. Take their kitchen, for instance. The refrigerator was the size of a queen-sized bed. The stove had so many burners you could cook a whole cow on top. The kitchen table was the size of a Jacuzzi tub.

Because it was supersized, it took a long time to cross through the hallway and the living room. The tile floor was very slippery, and I was tempted to take off my shoes and slide across, but I didn't. I probably would've knocked over one of the many supersized sculptures, or banged into the white, supersized piano or the supersized fish tank holding the super-sized tropical fish.

I followed the noise up the stairs to Brandon's bedroom, which was the size of our living room. He was surrounded by six other boys and playing a video game on a supersized TV. I didn't recognize any of the boys except Axel. He gave me his usual sneer. I figured that maybe the other kids were guys

Brandon knew from the neighborhood. I never found out, because Brandon never introduced me to them, and I didn't introduce myself, and no one introduced himself to me. My mom would've been very disappointed in all of us.

"Hey, Brandon, happy birthday," I said.

"Hey."

"Great party going on."

"Yeah, it's okay . . . aw man! I almost got that guy!" he groaned, waving his hand at the TV. I looked at the game box; he was playing DeathLord III: Ultra-Destruction. I don't know much about TV and movies, and I know even less about video games. It didn't look like that much fun compared with the sword jugglers and the camel rides and the live tiger, but I couldn't leave. Not yet. I didn't want to be rude to Brandon, and I didn't want Axel to think I felt out of place.

So I climbed up onto the supersized bed. Axel was slumped against the wall. He didn't look happy. Actually, none of the guys looked particularly happy, including Brandon. We all just sat, watching him play. Every once in a while someone would shout out, "Good one!" or "Watch out, there's a bomb on the left" or "Grab that health capsule, you're running low on life energy." Brandon had his window shades pulled down to reduce the glare on the television, but I could hear the music drifting in from the backyard, in between the gunfire, explosions, and death screams coming from the game.

"Hey, Brandon, I'm going to grab something to eat," I said. "Maybe I'll see you outside?"

"Yeah, sure," he said. I was pretty sure I wouldn't.

The line for the camels was pretty short. Riding a camel looked like a lot of fun, but what I really wanted to see was the tiger. It was easy to find; a small crowd of people surrounded the belly dancer who was leading it on a short chain leash. The belly dancer was very nicely but very firmly instructing people to keep their distance.

I slipped through the circle to the front, where I could get a better view. The tiger was young, and he was fascinated by his own tail. He kept trying to catch it in his paws, like a kitten. But he wasn't a kitten. He was a real, live tiger, and I was only three feet away from him!

A man wearing a khaki safari uniform stood to the side, holding the orangutan that had previously been with the belly dancer, and was answering people's questions. I hadn't seen him before because when there is a belly dancer with a tiger, who would pay any attention to a fat man in khaki? But soon I realized he was the official animal wrangler, and the belly dancers were his assistants.

"No, the animals are not tame," the man in khaki said in

answer to one question. "They will never be tame. They're *trained*. It's a big difference."

"Where did you get them?" I asked.

"We rescued the tiger. He'd been smuggled here from Asia and was being illegally kept as a pet. This little fellow on my shoulders is named Jeeves. I raised him from a baby. I bottle-fed him myself after his mother abandoned him."

"Do you work for the zoo?" someone asked.

"No, my company is called Animal Kingdom, Inc. We supply animals for movies all over the world—and private parties," he added as an afterthought.

"Are the cats dangerous?" someone else asked.

"Yes. Very. Don't let the leash fool you. All wild animals have the potential to be dangerous. That's why we ask you to keep your distance—not to hold food around them. Also, don't make any loud noises. The shrieking sounds of laughter can sound like the squeal of prey to them. . . . Excuse me, young man, would you please stand back three feet? No petting the animals. He can give you a pretty serious bite."

A teenager who had reached his hand out pulled it back. I wished he hadn't gotten that close, because the man in khaki seemed to use that as an excuse to leave.

"Sorry, folks, I can't leave these animals out too long. They get tired, just like you and me. But we've got a lot more in store for you. I have a desert fox and a chimpanzee waiting in the wings."

The man in khaki and his assistants led the animals out a side gate toward a five-car garage. I hadn't eaten anything yet, so I grabbed a plateful of food from the adult buffet tent (some really good roast chicken, a flat Mediterranean bread, and supersized almond cookies) and then turned and nearly ran into J.J.

"Oh, hi, Mitch, how long have you been here?"

"A little more than an hour," I said. I glanced around her to see if Tangie was with her, but she wasn't.

"I've been here right from the beginning," J.J. said, not noticing my glances. "My dad represents some of the guests, you know. He wants to schmooze."

"Schmooze?"

J.J. laughed. "I forgot you don't speak Hollywoodese. It means to socialize and conduct business at the same time."

"Doesn't your dad ever relax?"

"You snooze, you lose. Besides, ninety percent of the people here are here to schmooze. The other ten percent are serving drinks."

"My parents aren't here to schmooze. . . ."

"No, but *you* are." She had a strange gleam in her eye.

"Me?"

"Mitch. This backyard is full of writers, actors, directors, and producers. Not one is going to let an opportunity like this go by without trying to further their career, including you. Now get out there and talk to some people! My dad can only do so much—you've got to work the room too . . . or the yard, as the case may be."

"I can't just walk up to perfect strangers and butt into their conversation without them knowing me. . . ."

"Hello? Fizzy Whiz Kid? They *know* who you are!"

J.J. linked her arm in mine and led me to a group of adults. They stopped talking as we walked up, and a few smiled at me in recognition. Only one of them didn't: Axel's mom. She had the look of a deer about to bolt.

"Hello, everyone," J.J. said as though it were perfectly normal to interrupt adults. "I'd like to introduce my friend, Mitch Mathis. He's the Fizzy Whiz Kid."

"Oh, that's right," they responded all at once. "Yes, yes, from the World Series commercial." "You like bubbles?" "Very funny work."

"Mrs. Mulligan was actually the one who discovered Mitch," J.J. continued. "Isn't that right, Mrs. Mulligan?"

Axel's mom blinked for a second, and then, in an amazing transformation, all her frostiness melted away like a snowball on a hot sidewalk. She plastered a big ol' smile on her face and said, "That's right, J.J. Mitch came to one of our youth talent searches. He really stood out from the crowd. As soon as I saw him, I knew Mitch had it."

I looked at Mrs. Mulligan, shocked. What was she playing at? Then I noticed J.J. give me the same sly look her father had slipped me in my meeting with him. J.J. knew exactly what she was doing. She locked her arm back in mine.

"I just wanted to make sure you all met the next big character actor while you could still afford him." She laughed, tugging me away. The adults laughed too.

"Bye," I said, waving. "Nice to meet all of you." When we were some distance away I turned to J.J. "You're amazing."

"I know, but thank you."

"I thought Mrs. Mulligan hated me. . . ."

"She did. Axel told me all about how she got that lump on her head. But now she has the credit for your success. Now she *loves* you."

"It's that simple?"

"Nothing is simple in this town, Mitch. But getting credit for success can go a long way to mending fences." J.J. glanced around the yard. "So . . . did your parents come with you?"

"Yes . . . that's them, over there," I said as I noticed them come out from the dessert tent with a couple of plates piled with goodies. They waved to me and walked over. It didn't seem like J.J. was going anywhere; in fact, she seemed dead-set on meeting my folks. I couldn't believe it. Maybe Skywalker was right. Maybe J.J. really did have a crush on me.

EVIDENCE THAT J.J. HAS A CRUSH ON ME

1. Keeps helping me without my asking for it
2. Always looks at me in class, and when I catch her she makes a face
3. Helped herself to my dessert at lunch without asking, twice
4. Is excited to meet my parents
5. Asks a lot of nosy questions about my family life
6. Keeps touching me—put arm in mine, also shoved me in the back and stepped on my foot "by accident"

"Hi, Mitch," my mom said, walking up to us. "Is this one of your school friends?"

"Yes," I said, but before I could continue J.J. had already thrust her hand out.

"Hello, Mrs. Mathis," she chirped. "I'm J.J. Schwartz, Jeremy Schwartz's daughter. It really is a pleasure to meet you."

"Nice to meet you too, J.J.," my mom said, and before she

finished what she was going to say, J.J. had already turned to my dad.

"Hello, Mr. Mathis," J.J. continued. "I just loved your presentation in our classroom. Remember? The one about the cockroaches."

"Why, thank you," my dad said, surprised. I groaned silently. I'd hoped that was behind me by now, but J.J. just kept on going. She must really like me a lot, because she was sure trying to impress me by kissing up to my dad. While she was yakking away I took the opportunity to take a good look at her. Her ponytail bobbed up and down when she spoke, and she had a splatter of freckles on her nose and a way of raising one eyebrow whenever she didn't agree with what was going on. And she was smart, probably the smartest girl in the class. When she wasn't busy showing off, she could be kind of funny. I guess when it came down to it, she wasn't such a bad person to have adoring you.

"I'll see you later, Mitch," J.J. was saying. She had finished gushing over my parents and gave me a quick squeeze on the arm. Touching me, again!

"Yeah, I'll see you at school," I said with a wave.

"Well! She seemed nice," my dad said after she left.

"She's a lot like her father," my mom pointed out, in

between bites of honeyed cake. "So, you think you're ready to go, Mitch?"

I looked at my watch. We'd only been there for an hour and a half. I was about to protest, but then I realized I was ready to go. Now that J.J. was gone I couldn't see anyone else I wanted to talk to. There was still a lot of great stuff going on, and a lot of interesting things to look at, but you have to be real careful about standing around by yourself at a party; it doesn't look good. It's a clear sign that you are a big loser. Hanging out with your parents is also a no-no. I definitely wasn't going to go back to Brandon's room, I didn't want to wait out the line for the camel, I'd eaten, and I'd even schmoozed . . . a little. It was time to go.

Soon we were back in our car, winding our way back down to the flatlands. My parents didn't say much, but they both had funny looks on their faces. I wondered what they had been doing at the party while I was away.

That night Dad went to a video store and came home with an armload of movies and television series on DVD. After I went to bed, he and my mom stayed up late watching them. I didn't say anything, but I think after talking to the crowd at the party they were beginning to understand just what I had been going through at DeMille Elementary.

11

Welcome to the Jungle

THE NEXT DAY I GOT SOME BAD NEWS.
The second commercial was scheduled to shoot on the same day as the class field trip to the Jet Propulsion Laboratory. When I asked Jeremy if there was any way they could reschedule it, he just laughed.

"Mitch, Mitch, Mitch, haven't you ever heard the old saying 'The show must go on'? There are a lot of people invested in this commercial. Fizzy Whiz is getting ready to roll out an entire ad campaign! And they need you! The Fizzy Whiz Kid! Besides, JPL will always be there. Go some other time." Then he had to take another call.

I told Mrs. Samuelson that I wouldn't be able to go on the trip. She said she was sorry I couldn't make it, but she understood and would excuse the absence as long as I brought in a written note from my parents. "It must be very exciting to be part of a whole advertising campaign," she added. That made me feel a little better, but then Tangie made me feel worse.

"I heard you tell Mrs. Samuelson you aren't coming on the trip," she whispered as I sat down. "You're going to miss out on a lot. The planetarium show is amazing. I've seen it two times already. You can lose yourself in the stars."

The chance to be in a dark theater next to Tangie. . . . I *was* missing out on a lot.

I told Skywalker and Dash about the conflict after school while we were playing handball. Skywalker expressed his sympathies, but Dash just shrugged and said, "You gotta do what you gotta do." Dash had been acting a little weird ever since Brandon's birthday party. In fact, he seemed to take it personally whenever I even talked to Brandon. I hoped that hanging out with him and Skywalker after school would convince him that I hadn't been "lured to the dark side," to use a *Star Wars* phrase.

"It's the biggest field trip of the year," Skywalker continued, serving the ball. "I think the only other place we go to this year is the Natural History Museum, to look at minerals." He rolled his eyes and then faked a great big yawn. I took the opportunity to slam the ball as hard as I could. It ricocheted off the wall and arced over a group of little kids who were staring at us.

"I think the Fizzy Whiz fan club has arrived," Dash said sarcastically, nodding at the small group.

I looked over at the kids and waved. "Hey," I said. The kids ran off. I shrugged. I was beginning to get used to the extra attention. "Well, at least I know when all of the commercials are scheduled for the next few months. I'll just have to make sure I don't plan anything fun that would overlap with them."

"Are you doing anything on December fourth?" Dash said.

"I don't think so. What's happening December fourth?"

"It's just my birthday. I'm having a little party, just four or five guys. It's not going to be nearly as fantabulous or splendiferous as Brandon's party—"

"Will you stop?" I interrupted. Dash's attitude was really starting to bug me. "Brandon's party was not that great. Really. I left early. I only went because I was curious. . . ."

"Hey, you don't need to explain yourself to me," Dash said.

"I know, but I just want you to know why I went. I know who my real friends are."

That seemed to satisfy something in Dash's mind. "Yeah, well, we're going to a laser-tag arcade, and then everyone's going to sleep over."

"I'll be there," I said. "For sure."

The kids had come back and were slowly inching their way toward the handball courts. Dash rolled his eyes and jerked his thumb at them again.

"What is it, guys?" I said.

"Can we have your autograph?" one of them mumbled.

"Well, we're kind of in the middle of a game. . . ."

"No, Mitch, give it to them," Skywalker said quietly. "Give them a thrill. They'll remember it the rest of their lives."

"Oh, come on, that's ridiculous."

"I'm serious, man. It's nothing to you, just a few seconds, but it's going to mean a lot to them."

I shrugged and went over to them. None of them had a piece of paper, so I signed a candy wrapper, a piece of torn newspaper, and the bottom of one kid's T-shirt. It seemed pretty silly, but they couldn't have been happier.

Thursday morning my mom drove me to Warner Bros. Studios again for the second commercial shoot. On the way we passed by DeMille Elementary and I could see the yellow school bus parked in front, waiting to be boarded by the sixth-grade class. I couldn't believe I was going to miss the field trip! Why couldn't the commercial shoot have landed on a same day as a math test, or on the same day that we had to learn folk dancing in PE? That would've been much better!

Once we reached the studio, we pulled into my parking space. But my mom was just dropping me off; she had a meeting that day at the university, so a limousine would be taking me home. A limo! I'd never been in a limo before. When I was at my cousin's wedding, I saw the inside of one, though. It was really long, big enough to hold eight people, and it had a TV, colored neon lights, and a bar stocked with all kinds of drinks. There were also about twelve surround-sound speakers pumping the bride's and groom's favorite tunes. Sweet.

Brandy greeted us as soon as we got out of the car.

"Thank you, Mrs. Mathis," she said. "I'll take Mitch from here. And don't worry—we'll keep an eye on him. He's with the teacher all day unless he's on the set."

Teacher? No one said anything about a teacher! My mom noticed my surprise and gave me one of her looks that said very clearly, *Mind your manners.* Then she wrote something on a piece of paper and handed it to the production assistant.

"If you need me, I'm at this number," she said. "Have fun, Mitch." She climbed into her car and took off.

"We're going to a really cool part of the backlot—it's called 'the jungle,'" Brandy said, leading me along a path.

The jungle was still being prepared for the commercial.

People were setting up lights and cameras, and Alvin was right in the middle of everything, firing off orders like a machine gun. Brandy led me to a long, white camper with two doors in it.

"This is your dressing room," Brandy said, pointing at the door with my name written in marker on masking tape. "And this other door is to your classroom."

She knocked on the second door, then opened it. I followed her inside. The room was pretty empty: just a counter, a couple of chairs, and a very small woman—a little person—reading a newspaper. She had bright orange hair fashioned into a beehive hairdo. Her pink lipstick matched her pink nails, but nothing matched her leopard-print pantsuit. She peered at me from behind pink rhinestone glasses.

"Maureen, this is Mitch," Brandy said. "Mitch, this is your tutor, Maureen Koslowski."

"Nice to meet you," I said, trying not to stare. But it was hard. She was possibly the oddest-looking person I've ever seen.

"Likewise," she said in a gravelly voice.

"Well! I'll leave you two alone. I'll come get you when we're ready for you on the set, Mitch." Brandy gave me a little wave as she closed the door behind her. Maureen tilted her head down and looked at me over her glasses.

"I bet you didn't expect me," she said. "Nobody does." She pointed at the other stool at the counter, so I took a seat. "I bet you're thinking, 'She sure doesn't look like a teacher—there must be some mistake,' right?"

That's exactly what I was thinking, but I didn't want to offend her, so I gave a sort of vague shrug.

"Well, you're not wrong. I haven't always been a teacher. Look, kid, I've been bumpin' around this burg a long time. You want to know how I lasted so long? Flexibility. I've had all kinds of gigs in this town. I've been a secretary, an actress, an acrobat, a stand-in, a stunt double, a voice actor. . . . Now I'm your teacher."

"I didn't really expect to have school today," I admitted. Maureen twisted her bright pink lips into a wry sort of smile.

"Sorry to have to break the bad news to you, bub, but whenever there's a kid on the set, you need a teacher on the set. State law. Nothing we can do about it. So let's start off on the right foot. First, don't mangle my last name. Don't even try to say it. Just call me 'Mo.' Second, I do not like being stared at. I also don't like when people avoid looking at me, like you're doing right now. Third, I don't want your help getting things off shelves. If you even think of lifting me I will bite you. Fourth, no, I did not appear in *The Wizard of Oz*, so don't ask. Fifth, I take this job seriously. You are going to do real academic work.

Show business isn't all fun and games. Nobody likes a stupid actor, least of all me. Think you can handle that?"

"Yes, ma'am . . . I mean, Mo."

"Good. Let's start with math." She pushed a book toward me. "Do the word problems on page one hundred and twelve, and then we'll talk."

The morning dragged by slowly. Once we finished with math, Mo had a short story she wanted me to read, and then I had to write a paragraph analyzing it. I kept waiting for Brandy to come back and tell me that they were ready for me on the set, but it didn't happen. At noon Mo looked at her watch and slid off the stool. She was taller sitting than she was standing. "Time for lunch," she said, and she headed out the door.

As we left the backlot, Mo trudged ahead of me by several paces, even though her legs were half the length of mine. I had to jog to keep up with her.

"What's taking Alvin so long?" I said. "I thought I'd be on the set and maybe even finished by now."

"Hah! That's show business for you," Mo snorted. "It's a lot of 'hurry up and wait.' I bet if I added up all the time I've wasted just sitting on my *tuchus* waiting to say one or two lines, it would add up to years!"

We passed the soundstage with the pirates' treasure cave

inside, and the door was open a crack. Mo noticed my gaze linger in that direction.

"You want to take a peek?" she said. I nodded. "We're really not supposed to go in here," Mo warned, but she was tugging on my arm, pulling me inside.

Nobody was on the soundstage; we had it all to ourselves. We picked our way along a path around the lagoon, which hadn't been drained yet, and then climbed up the mountain of gold coins, plates, and candelabra. There were also swords, pistols, and chests filled with gems scattered around, along with a few pirate skeletons. Mo plunked herself down on a gilded throne and lifted up a sword.

"Shiver me timbers," she growled. I laughed. She gestured with her sword at a saber that was a few feet away from me. I picked it up, along with the pirate hat that was next to it.

"Avast, ye scurrilous dog!" I shouted back, pointing my sword at her.

Mo leaped to her feet. "Ye will regret those words, sniveling water rat!" She swung her sword with surprising forcefulness, catching me completely off guard. I managed to block her first attack, but she kept coming at me, parrying, thrusting, twirling, and I quickly figured out that Mo knew how to fence. She was better than Skywalker with his broomstick. It's a good thing the swords were fake, because otherwise I'd be meat loaf.

After a few minutes I got tired of being poked and dropped my sword. Mo thrust hers into a mound of gold coins.

"Now I've really worked up an appetite," she said. "Let's grab some grub." We picked our way back along the lagoon path and out into the sunlight.

"Back in the olden days directors would shoot just about everything on soundstages, or on the backlot," Mo explained. "These days audiences expect everything to look real, so now directors shoot on location. That means everyone involved in the production has to pack up and travel to wherever the movie or TV show is being shot, whether it's in the desert, the Arctic, or, if you're lucky, Paris. It's expensive, though. Using the backlot is much cheaper."

"What about that building?" I said, pointing at a long building that looked like a Spanish mission.

"That's where the suits work . . . I mean the executives." Mo led me up the stairs of a low, flat building. "Here's the commissary." I must have looked confused because she then added, "That's a showbiz word for 'cafeteria.'"

We got in line to get our food. I reached to get a plate of green Jell-O for Mo, and she kicked me in the shin, hard. I yelled and pulled my hand back. Mo got her own Jell-O. Then we sat down at one of the tables.

While we were eating lunch, we saw the entire cast of *Kick the Bride* come in, joking around with each other and waving to other people they knew. Then Monty Montgomery entered with someone who looked a lot like Jeremy Schwartz. It was, in fact, Jeremy Schwartz, and they very casually slid into a side room with a glass door, which Mo, sniffing, said was the private dining room "for the high muckety-mucks."

Brandy intercepted us on our way back to the trailer and told us they were ready for a rehearsal. Mo went back to the trailer to make a phone call, and I went with Brandy to the jungle set, which still wasn't completely ready. I found out then that there had been a technical problem and we probably wouldn't get to shoot the commercial until tomorrow. I was so mad. I was missing the field trip for nothing!

Each of the next five Fizzy Whiz commercials was going to have its own theme. This one had a jungle theme, the next would be a western, then pirates, science fiction, and finally horror. My line in each movie was the same line I had in the first commercial—"You like bubbles?"—but in each one my entrance would be different.

In this commercial, Tarzan saves Jane from dangerous headhunters. They fight, Tarzan defeats them, and then he and Jane celebrate with some soda. They open their cans and the soda is flat. Then I'm supposed to swing in on a vine and say, "You like bubbles?" I open the soda. It squirts Tarzan in the face. Jane laughs. Tarzan opens his soda and squirts Jane in the face. They both laugh and enjoy their refreshing drink. One of the headhunters returns. I open a can of soda for him, squirting him, he looks angry, and then he laughs and joins Tarzan and Jane. The end.

I was happy to see that Edward, the funny actor from the first commercial, was going to play the headhunter. It turns out they liked him so much they made a five-commercial deal with him as well.

We read through the script a few times until Alvin was satisfied. It's funny how I felt much more relaxed this time. I didn't feel I had to prove anything since I'd already done it once before. On top of that, I recognized so many people who were on the set that it was like visiting old friends.

After we finished the "read-through," Alvin started working with Tarzan and Jane. A fight choreographer showed them how to make the fight look realistic, blow by blow. It was almost like learning a dance. It was interesting to watch . . . for a while. Then I got bored. I could see what Mo meant by "hurry up and wait." I was back to waiting.

To pass the time I pestered Brandy with questions about what jobs everyone did on the set. I made a list of the weird ones so that I could remember them.

WEIRD JOB TITLES

- Gaffer: The chief lighting technician
- Best boy: The chief assistant lighting technician
- Grip: A person responsible for setup, adjustment, and maintenance of equipment on the set
- Key grip: The chief of a group of grips
- Craft services: The person who provides snacks for people working on the set
- Boom operator: The person who works the boom, which is a long pole with a microphone on the end of it

"Do I know you from somewhere?" a voice behind me said. I turned. It was the man in khaki from Animal Kingdom. Only now he was wearing jeans and a leather jacket.

"I asked you a question at a birthday party," I said. "Brandon Goldwyn's party."

The man rolled his eyes. "Oh, *that* party. Did you have a good time?"

"Not really," I admitted.

"Neither did my assistants," he said, laughing. "My name is Perry, by the way." He extended his hand, which I shook.

"Mitch Mathis," I said. And then I blurted out, "You've got a way-cool job!"

Perry laughed. "Yeah? I guess it is way cool." He scratched his head, and then his eyes brightened. "Hey, you want to meet Betsy? She's the Bengal tiger we're using in this shoot. She's a lot bigger than the little guy I brought to the party."

"Oh boy, would I!" I said, jumping off my director's chair.

Perry led me a short distance from the set to a huge truck that held several large cages. From the largest cage I could hear a loud purring that sounded like a motor.

"Here she is," Perry said proudly.

I peeked inside the cage. At the back, in the shadows, lay the tiger. She watched me carefully, purring the entire time. "Are you going to take her out for the rehearsal?"

"No. We're going to shoot her on her own and then edit her in. She's just window dressing—all she has to do is sit there. I have a different tiger for action work. Betsy's really only good at looking big."

I noticed an orangutan in a smaller cage. "Is that Jeeves?"

"Ah, yes, you remember Jeeves," Perry said. He opened the cage and Jeeves immediately scrambled out and up Perry's legs, finally landing on his shoulder.

"Jeeves is probably the smartest animal I've ever worked with," Perry said. "Usually when you try to teach an animal a trick, it takes months. I once had to train ducks to walk across a stage, pick up pieces of paper, and swim away with them.

Man, that's eight months of my life I'll never have back. Jeeves can learn something in an afternoon." At this moment Jeeves was carefully inspecting Perry's hair.

"How do you teach him to do anything?"

"Generally I use a reward system. Like, let's say a scene calls for a bear to stand on its hind legs on cue. I'd start by flashing a light at him and getting him to stand by holding a treat over his head. When I get him to do it once, I reward him right away with a treat. Each time he repeats the desired behavior, I reward him. Pretty soon it gets to the point where as soon as that light goes off the bear stands because he's looking forward to the treat. That's when you're ready to shoot."

"So it's like training a dog."

"Yes, but each animal is different. Some are definitely smarter than others. You can teach apes and dogs to do all kinds of things. Other animals have such simple brains you have to work with their instincts."

"Is it hard?" I asked.

"Well, that depends. It takes a certain kind of person to train animals, someone who can read an animal's body language, someone who has a feel for them—knows them inside and out. And you have to be patient. Very patient."

"I'm pretty good at reading people," I said. "And I always seem to know what my dog wants."

"A wild animal isn't a dog. You see this?" Perry held up his hand. For the first time I noticed he had lost part of his ring finger, right above the first knuckle. "That got bitten off by an angry chimp, and I was lucky she didn't take more. That's what can happen if you make a mistake."

"And you still do it? You still train animals, even after . . . after that?" I asked, pointing at his finger.

"I can't help it," Perry said with a grin. "I've got the show-business bug."

12
King of the Hill

THE LIMOUSINE THAT TOOK ME HOME wasn't at all like my cousin's limo. It was just a big black four-door sedan with a driver. The driver didn't have a chauffeur's cap, but he was wearing a suit and sunglasses. There wasn't a TV either, or neon lights, but somebody had put a nice cold root beer in the cup holder. The limo was still very, very cool. Whenever we stopped at a red light, people on the sidewalk casually tried to look through the tinted windows to see who I was. *The Fizzy Whiz Kid*, I thought to myself. *I'm the Fizzy Whiz Kid, that's who I am!*

By the next day the technical problems had been solved, and we shot the commercial. I didn't get to swing on the vine after all, as that was considered a "stunt," so my "stunt double," a short, forty-year-old man wearing a wig, filled in. I was still hoisted into the tree to say my line, though, and they lifted me up with a safety harness. From the ground it didn't look like the tree branch was that high, but once I was up there it was pretty scary. It took five takes for me to say the line without looking down, and two more for me to say it with a believable smile. I was happy when it was over and I was back on the ground.

Once I was finished it was Betsy's turn. I watched as Perry handled the huge Bengal tiger through her part of the shoot; all he had to do was get her to lie on a platform in Tarzan's tree house and then roar on cue. While Perry was working he let me take care of Jeeves, who was fascinated by my Fizzy Whiz cap. Jeeves kept snatching it off my head and throwing it, and then after I picked it up and brought it back, he would do it all over again. It was like playing fetch, only I guess I was the dog.

After Betsy finished her part, Perry didn't stick around. He had another job, so he loaded up his truck and left. I couldn't leave, because I had to be there in case Alvin wanted to reshoot, so I was back to waiting. I found myself seeking out Mo.

I found her in the classroom trailer playing solitaire. She was wearing another wacky outfit: a yellow sweater with three huge buttons and a feather ruffle along the collar and a pair of plaid leggings.

"I was wondering when you were going to show up," she said, gathering up the cards. She did a series of fancy shuffles, fluttering the cards from one hand to the other. She smiled that crooked smile of hers, showed me the top card, put it back, tapped the deck, and revealed the first card: It had changed. Then she spread the deck smoothly in a line, flipped the first card, and it pushed the rest over like dominoes.

"Wow! How did you . . . ?"

"I was also a card dealer in Vegas," she said, gathering the cards again. "These are special cards, made for little hands." She tucked the cards in her sweater and turned back to me. "Now, you have a choice. We can do math or social studies. If I were you, I'd pick social studies." She had a twinkle in her eye. I picked social studies.

"Good choice. Time for a field trip," she said, and she slipped off the stool and headed out the door.

"Where are we going?" I asked, trying to keep up with her.

"Social studies is the study of your community, isn't it? Well, let's take a look at the community."

We hopped on a golf cart and sped off the backlot, past the soundstages, to an area that had several buildings that looked like warehouses. "This is where all the preproduction work gets done," Mo yelled to me. "Construction, props, lighting, costumes, makeup, all that kind of stuff. Hold on." She veered down an alley and up to the costume department, the same place I had been fitted for my Fizzy Whiz Kid outfit. As we entered, Mo waved off the receptionist, who seemed to know better than to try to stop her as we charged past. Then we went through the same hallway I'd seen before, past several dressing rooms similar to the one I'd already been in.

When we got to the end of the hall, Mo pushed open the door, and I followed her inside. I found myself standing in a warehouse, surrounded by hundreds of racks of clothing, row after row after row, extending as far as the eye could see. The racks rose up four levels high so that you would need a pretty tall ladder to reach the outfits at the top. The costumes seemed to be organized by theme: historical, wedding, science fiction and fantasy, clothing from different cultures, and even regular clothes that you'd find people wearing on the street.

"They have every single piece of clothing here catalogued, from every last Victorian bloomer to every last belt," she said proudly. I could tell this was one of her favorite places. "And they have costumes from movies as far back as the nineteen twenties, worn by some of the greats," she added. "Humphrey Bogart, James Cagney, Vivien Leigh, Lauren Bacall . . ."

"Who?" I asked.

Mo gave me an annoyed look. "I bet you've never even seen a movie that's in black and white," she said. I didn't have the heart to tell her that I had only seen *Star Wars* a month ago. That would probably have sent her right over the edge.

While we were standing there, I noticed a line of gladiator costumes. The one I was looking at was made of thick leather strips and pads and held together with some kind of studs.

"Wow, this is really heavy," I said, trying to lift it off the rack.

"You bet it is. A realistic costume helps an actor get into character. Gladiators had to wear thick leather armor. It was all they had between themselves and the sharp end of a sword, a spear, or even a lion's jaws." Mo then went on to describe how most gladiators were Roman slaves trained to fight to the death in an arena called a colosseum as entertainment for the Roman citizens. That led her to describe the ancient Roman government and their society, and then to talk about Julius Caesar and his nephew, Augustus Caesar, the first and greatest emperor of Rome. By the time she finished, I realized we'd been in the warehouse for an hour.

"C'mon," Mo said. "That's enough history. Next time I'll tell you about the Egyptians. We have a great collection of gorgeous Cleopatra costumes."

Suddenly she was up again and on the move. Before I could catch up, Mo had already disappeared through the swinging doors.

I ran into the next room. It contained a bunch of sewing

machines, each with a costumer behind it, whirring away. It was incredibly noisy, like a factory floor. At a fitting area an actress modeled a costume while a costumer pinned it up. I had no idea what it was going to be used for, but it looked like a wedding dress for an octopus. I saw a flash of yellow and plaid zip through the door across the room.

Once I stepped through that door I was in a different hallway lined with offices. Mo was way ahead of me. I wished she'd slow down. I would've liked to explore a little longer, but then we were out the door, back in the bright sunlight.

"That was fantastic!" I said. "I wish we hadn't rushed through the rest of those rooms. What the heck was that model trying on anyway . . . ?" It was then that I noticed Mo was wearing something new: a rhinestone-studded jacket. "Where did you get that?"

"You like it?" she said, twirling around.

"Did you just . . . swipe that?"

"'Swipe' is such a strong word. Let's just say I borrowed it," she said. "You can't find stuff like this in stores anymore." I must've been frowning, because she added, "Hey, it's cold today! I needed a jacket! I'll bring it back tomorrow. Now come on, the field trip's not over."

The next place we visited was the property department, and in many ways it was similar to the costume department in that it was also a huge warehouse. Instead of costumes, though, it held every kind of furniture imaginable, from stuff that looked like it was put together by pioneers to futuristic bubble chairs. Chandeliers, rugs, paintings, and hundreds of knickknacks filled the rooms.

"Wow, are these antiques?" I asked. We had stopped inside a room with a lot of pioneer furniture—rustic chairs, tables, and beds with lumpy mattresses.

"Some of them are, but a lot of this stuff is just built and then distressed—that means it's made to look old. They're set dressing. They don't have to work, they just have to make the set look believable. Props are the items on the set that an actor actually uses during a scene. Those do have to work. Like this."

Mo sat on a bench that had a big wheel attached to it. "You know what this is?" I shook my head. "It's a spinning wheel." I guess it must've been obvious I didn't know what she was talking about because she tilted her head and looked at me over her glasses. "You know, a spinning wheel? Like in 'Rumpelstiltskin,' spinning straw into gold? Or 'Sleeping Beauty'? The gal who pricked her finger on the spindle of a spinning wheel and fell into a deep sleep?"

"Ohhh, yeah, a spinning wheel . . ."

"Well, those stories are fantasy. This is the real thing. And it doesn't spin straw into gold or put you to sleep. It spins wool fleece into yarn that the pioneers used to make warm clothes and blankets."

That was the beginning of a whole other lesson about pioneers and their struggle to survive on the harsh frontier as Americans spread westward in the nineteenth century. Mo showed me some smaller pioneer props: apple-head dolls, tops, tin plates, and a cradle hollowed out of a log. Again, she went on for about forty-five minutes before she looked at her watch.

"Oh my," she said. "We've been yakking here like we've got all the time in the world, but it's time for you to go home."

"I don't mind coming home late. . . ."

"Not on my watch, bub. This particular job I'd like to keep for a while."

We walked to the parking lot. I kept peppering Mo with questions about what we'd seen, but I didn't get answers to all of them, because the limo was already there, waiting for me.

As it pulled out of the lot I felt a little depressed. It was like spending all day at an amusement park and then heading home, knowing that when you get there you'll be faced with a bunch of chores. So much had happened that day. I'd seen a forty-year-old man pretend to be me. I'd seen a Bengal tiger roar. I'd played fetch with an orangutan. I'd been an accomplice in the theft of a rhinestone jacket. And I'd learned a heck of a lot of history.

"Hey, will you look at that!" the driver said suddenly.

I looked out the window. There, among the huge billboards overlooking Sunset Boulevard, was a new one, but this one had a familiar face. Mine! My big head was four stories high, grinning over Sunset Boulevard with a can of soda next to it and the words FIZZY WHIZ SODA, and then on the next line, YOU LIKE BUBBLES?

"That's you, isn't it?" the driver said.

"It sure is," I said proudly.

My mom had seen the billboard. My dad had seen the billboard. The next day at school it seemed as if everyone had either seen the billboard or knew about it. That problem I had at the beginning of the year, when I was in danger of being a major loser? Ancient history.

When I walked into the grocery store, I'd hear, "Hey, it's the Fizzy Whiz Kid!" When I went to the park, I'd hear, "Look, the Fizzy Whiz Kid!" When I rode my bike, "Hey, you like bubbles?" When we went out to a restaurant, "It's the kid on the billboard! The Fizzy Whiz Kid!" I was signing so many autographs I went through five pens in a week.

The second commercial aired over Thanksgiving weekend. After that I got another invitation to go to Brandon's house. At first I wasn't going to go. Brandon's birthday party hadn't been much fun—it had just been bizarre. But my mom thought it was rude of me to turn down the invitation, so I went.

Brandon had a real butler who served us snacks on a silver tray. We went swimming in his pool. We raced each other down the slides and did crazy flips off the diving board. We played battleship using his supersized floats and supersized water guns. By "we" I mean Brandon's buddies and me. Brandon just hung out in his Jacuzzi playing some kind of hand-held game device.

I didn't see Axel there. I think he was avoiding me. He seemed to avoid me at school too. Any time somebody mentioned the billboard or the commercial, he would roll his eyes.

"Mitch Mathis isn't really doing anything a monkey couldn't do," I overheard him say more than once. "People are going to get tired of his face real fast. I know I already am."

J.J. hung around me more than ever. Every day she had a new piece of advice for me on how to navigate the mean streets of Hollywood.

J.J.'S TIPS FOR INCREASING STAR POWER

1. Don't do anything criminal or embarrassing, like shoplifting, trashing a hotel room, or going

swimming at the beach naked. You'll find yourself on the cover of every rag magazine in the grocery store, in a fuzzy, unflattering photo.

2. Find a charity to support. It'll make you seem caring. There are all kinds of diseases—just pick one and start talking about it.

3. Get a celebrity girlfriend. Not a real girlfriend, just somebody to be seen with.

4. Write a children's picture book.

5. Come up with a personal project, close to your heart, that you want to direct.

Most of this advice I ignored.

The only trouble was that with all this new popularity I didn't have as much time for Dash or Skywalker. Skywalker was cool about it, and in fact he would sometimes join conversations I was having with Brandon and J.J. or he'd hang out with us at lunch, but I didn't see much of Dash at all. He had stopped playing handball with Skywalker and me because autograph hounds would constantly interrupt our games. When we walked home he always found a reason to take a different route.

I hate to say this, but I think he was jealous.

I happened to mention this theory to Tangie. I thought she

might have some insight on this situation, and I was hoping for some sympathy, but Tangie just tilted her head in that way that she does and told me she didn't think Dash was jealous at all; he just didn't like the new role I was playing.

"I didn't create the character," I protested. "The Fizzy Whiz Company did."

"Not the Fizzy Whiz Kid," Tangie corrected. "I'm talking about the role of the fatheaded flavor of the month."

"Huh?"

"Look, Mitch, we all play roles in life. Shakespeare once wrote that 'all the world's a stage,' and during our lifetimes we play many parts. I think that's true. Skywalker is the artistic rebel. Dash is the intellectual. J.J. is the information power broker. Brandon is the spoiled millionaire. Axel . . . well, Axel used to be the obnoxious star, but that seems to be changing. And you've been changing roles constantly. When you first got here, you were the outsider. Then you became the apprentice. Now you're . . . well, you've become something else." She gave me a tight smile and then got up and walked away without looking back. What was that all about? I'd never heard Tangie be so direct. Then it dawned on me.

She was jealous too. That had to be it. Maybe she had tried to be an actress like her parents and couldn't cut it, and she was annoyed that all this fame just fell in my lap. Or maybe she was jealous of J.J.'s crush on me, which meant *she* had a crush on me too. Which was fantastic, except now she was mad at me. Things were getting very complicated.

Then the call came: the phone call from Jeremy that sent everything spinning out of control. He phoned at dinnertime, of course, because that was when he always called. "Get ready for the biggest night of your young life," Jeremy said without introducing himself. He didn't need to. "I just booked you on the hottest venue in Hollywood. You sitting down?"

"No . . ."

"Well, sit! I'm about to rock your adolescent world!"

I wasn't near a chair, so I sat on the floor. "Okay, I'm ready."

"Jeremy Schwartz, agent extraordinaire, has just landed you a role on the number one sitcom in America, *Kick the Bride*."

"Hey, that's great!"

"Great? That's all you can say? That's the best you can do? My God, Mitch, it's stupendous! Unbelievable! A miracle! And no audition, my little friend—it's yours. This is the next step in your career, Mitch, a *real* acting job. This is where you prove that you're more than just a funny-looking kid with a catchphrase. And it's filmed in front of a live audience. When those people see you walk out onstage, they're going to go nuts! Next Friday, December fourth, is going to be a night you'll remember for the rest of your life!"

My stomach sank. December fourth: Dash's birthday.

"Does it have to be on the fourth?" I moaned. "I don't think I can do it."

"What? Hold on, I don't think I heard you right, my ears are playing tricks on me. I thought I heard you say you don't think you can do it."

"It's just that there's something else I really wanted to do. . . ."

"Mitch, Mitch, you've *got* to do it. I raised hell to get you this deal. I cussed out too many people. You want me to go back to them now and say, 'Sorry, my mistake, we don't want the fame and fortune'? I can tell you now, that will be a poor career move."

"But I promised a friend I'd go to his birthday party."

"A birthday party? Good grief! That's what this is about? There will be many, many birthday parties, my little friend, but the chance for a debut on the number one hit show on primetime television? That does not come your way very often. Most actors would kill for this opportunity! They would literally murder somebody and risk the death penalty to be on this show."

"But I promised . . ."

"Hey, if he's really your friend he'll understand that this is more important. A real friend doesn't stand in the way of a friend's success. You hear what I'm saying? *I'm* your friend, and I want to see you do well. Right? That's how friendship works."

Jeremy was making a lot of sense. Dash should understand that this kind of opportunity doesn't come often. I *had* to take it. You snooze, you lose. My mom had entered the room, drawn by the volume of Jeremy's voice. She watched me, arms crossed.

"Let me talk to him," she mouthed. I nodded and handed her the phone.

"Hello? Mr. Schwartz . . . yes, Jeremy, this is Helen." My mom was using her no-nonsense voice. I could hear Jeremy start his news flash all over again, telling her to sit down, but she wasn't in the mood for his shenanigans.

I walked out of the room, sat at the dining room table, and waited with my dad, listening to the conversation. Five minutes later my mom hung up and came back in the room.

"Listen, Mitch," she said, sitting down. "You don't have to do anything that you don't want to do. Don't let that man pressure you. He's very good at his job, and he talks a good game. But it's *your* life, and you still have the power to say no."

"I know."

"He always calls at dinnertime," my dad said. "I told him not to call between six and seven—I explained in detail how we like to keep our meals uninterrupted, but he continues to call precisely at six thirty anyway. Then I realized why—he knows we're at home. He doesn't care about the inconvenience or about how sacred we feel our mealtimes are. He only cares about making deals. Remember that, Mitch: He's obsessed with his business, not with your well-being."

"Dad, he *does* care about my well-being. I know he's mainly interested in making money, and he gets a percentage of my income. But being on *Kick the Bride* really *is* a great opportunity for me."

"An opportunity that is getting in the way of something else that's important to you," my mom cut in.

"But I can always fix things with Dash," I said. "Guest starring on a top sitcom comes once in a lifetime."

"You don't know that," my mom argued. "Mitch, sometimes you can't have it both ways. Now, we're going to leave the decision up to you, and we'll support whatever you decide to do, but remember this: A person's character is no more or less than the choices he makes. You have to figure out what is important to *you*."

That night I thought about what my mom had said. It was obvious that she wanted me to turn Jeremy down. She didn't like Jeremy, she didn't trust him, she didn't like that he always called during dinner, and she was getting tired of my missing school. Even though I had kept my grades up, it didn't matter—she thought it was reinforcing bad habits and fostering a disregard for education. (I didn't pick all of that up from her expression—I overheard her saying it to my dad. The walls in our house are paper thin.)

But she didn't understand my side of it. She didn't know what it felt like to have people smiling at you all the time, to be recognized by strangers for something you'd done, to have little kids look up to you, and most of all how much fun it was to be part of creating stories to entertain people, even if those stories were only three minutes long and revolved around selling soda. I liked what I was doing, a lot.

I was going to take her at her word. She said it was my choice, and even though Jeremy was what she sometimes called a "shark," that didn't make him wrong. This *was* a great opportunity for me, and it probably wouldn't come again, especially if I turned it down this time. "If you're hot, you're hot, if you're not, you're not," J.J. would say over and over, sounding just like her dad. Right now, for whatever reason, I was hot, and if I didn't take advantage of it, I was closing the door on my future in show business.

The next morning I told my mom what I'd decided. She

gave me one of her disappointed smiles, but my mom rarely goes back on a promise (that would be bad manners), so I knew I was in the clear.

At school I pulled Dash aside after music class and told him the bad news, about my having to miss his birthday party. He took it better than I thought.

"It's all right," he said, shrugging.

"You know, I only have to do one scene," I said. "I bet I can get out of there early and still make it to the slumber party part of your party."

"Whatever," Dash said. "Look, Mitch, I can tell where I rank on your friend list. I've accepted it and moved on." He hitched his backpack on his shoulder and walked in the other direction, even though we were going back to the same classroom. I just stood there. I felt like I'd just been kicked in the stomach.

"Don't worry about it," Skywalker said, slapping me on the shoulder. He had witnessed the whole conversation. "Dash always takes things personally. He'll come around." I was beginning to realize that Skywalker was always optimistic, even when all signs pointed to disaster. The truth was, Dash was simply not acting like my friend anymore. He had stopped calling and e-mailing me, he didn't hang out at lunch, and I couldn't remember the last real conversation I'd had with him.

Maybe Jeremy was right. Maybe Dash wasn't a true friend after all.

When I got the script for *Kick the Bride*, I was a little disappointed. All of Jeremy's talk about this being the next step in my career had gotten my hopes up. I only had one line, in the second to last scene. I was supposed to be an annoying kid at a carnival, and at some point I was supposed to turn around, point a bubble gun at the star of the show, and say— you guessed it—"You like bubbles?" It was just a throwaway joke, but pretty funny in the context of the show.

My mom was not happy to hear that I would miss three days of school for rehearsals, Wednesday through Friday. The tutor on the *Kick the Bride* set was not nearly as interesting as Mo. She had a deep and personal love of geography, so that's what I studied for three days. Fortunately I didn't have to stay very late since my part was so small.

Taping a TV show was very different from working on a commercial. Instead of just one camera, there were four. One of the cameramen told me that three were shooting at all times while the fourth was setting up for a new shot. One camera might have a close-up of one character, another camera would have a close-up of a different character, and the third camera would have a wide shot of the whole scene. That way the director could cut back and forth between cameras, practically editing the show as it was being shot.

Having an audience watch the taping made a big difference too. You could feel the excitement coming from the hundreds of people in the stands, and you knew that if you made a mistake it would be in front of a crowd. When they laughed it felt like a wave of energy rushing over you. Sometimes a sign over the audience flashed, telling them when they were supposed to laugh. That was a little weird. I mean, couldn't they figure out when they were supposed to laugh themselves?

I didn't get a chance to hang out with the cast much; my mom kept me from wandering too far. She has very strong opinions about the appropriateness of a twelve-year-old chumming around with twentysomethings. On the day of the taping, she and I hung around the craft services table for a while and watched them tape the show from the TV monitor in my dressing room.

Finally the first assistant director knocked on my door and hustled me to where I would make my entrance. Walking backstage behind the scenery wasn't easy. There were hundreds of cables on the floor, and I had to be sure not to trip over them.

I got to my place. I heard my cue, and I walked out onto the stage to my mark. As soon as the audience recognized me they started laughing and whistling. I didn't expect that. There was so much noise I almost forgot to say my line. But then I remembered.

"You like bubbles?" I said. Huge laugh. Huge. I felt a rush like I'd never felt before, and at that moment I felt as if I would do anything to have that feeling again.

After I finished my part of the scene, I went back to my dressing room, where my mom was waiting. "That was a surprise," she said, but I could barely hear her because the blood in my head was still pounding.

At the end of the show the cast took their bows in front of the audience, and again I was brought out to cheers and whistles. I couldn't stop grinning. I had totally made the right choice in doing the show. I couldn't wait to tell Dash and Skywalker at the slumber party.

But I hadn't accounted for the "pickups." A pickup is when you have to reshoot a few lines because the director isn't happy with what he has "in the can." We waited for the audience to leave before we started the pickups, and that took some time. The director started with my scene, but we did three takes, so my mom and I didn't actually get to our car until ten. It was ten thirty by the time we got home. I raced to pack, quickly throwing clothes into a duffel bag, but my mom stopped me.

"Mitch, I don't think you can go to the party." As soon as

she said it, I realized she was right. I had missed it: the laser tag, the dinner, and the movie. If we left now, I'd probably arrive just in time for lights out.

My mom called Dash's mom, and she confirmed that it was probably best if I didn't come. She was sorry I hadn't been able to make it. My mom told her I would bring my birthday gift for Dash to school on Monday . . . which meant I had to remember to get one. In all the excitement I had forgotten.

13

A Cold Winter in L.A.

Dash blowing up at me. He never did. I had bought a really cool graphic novel collection for him from the comic book store, and I had an apology all ready, but when he walked into class he just said, "Oh hey, Mitch, sorry you couldn't make it to the party," and then he did something I'd never seen him do before. He passed my desk, walked over to Axel, and started up a conversation with him!

I just put the gift on his desk and sat down in my seat. Skywalker showed up a few minutes later.

"Oh man, did you miss a good time," he said, sliding into his chair. "I got the high score in laser tag, naturally. It's not that different from the guns they use in *Star Wars*. . . . What's wrong? You look like you've been hit with a brick."

"I . . . what's that all about?" I said, nodding in Dash's direction. He and Axel were now laughing about something that had to be hilarious, the way they were carrying on.

"Oh. That. Well, since you couldn't make it to the party, Dash invited Axel to take your place. He'd already paid for your laser tag ticket, and he didn't want to waste it."

"Well, who else was there?"

"Let's see . . . Dash, me, Axel, Tangie, J.J. . . . The girls didn't stay the night, of course. They left at about ten, after we watched the movie J.J. brought over. She had an early screener of the new James Bond movie. It is off-the-hook awesome! It's not coming out till Christmas. I don't know how she got it—her dad, I guess."

"Yeah, probably . . ." I glanced over at Dash and Axel yukking it up. I couldn't stand it anymore. "I thought Dash hated Axel's guts! When did you guys start hanging out?"

"Dash doesn't hate Axel, he just never said much to him because he was always with Brandon. Axel's not so bad, not really. He's started playing handball with us."

"What? You guys play without me?"

"Well, yeah, sometimes. You're so busy and all. . . .

Hey, did you know I got permission from the recreation center to paint murals on their handball courts?"

"No, I didn't know. When did that happen?"

"A while ago. I thought I told you. Anyway, Dash was helping me set up the paints, and Axel happened to be there. He really dug what I was doing, and told me so, and he was being so friendly and all, so Dash asked him if he wanted to play on one of the courts that I hadn't painted yet. He's actually got some pretty sweet moves."

I felt like an orphan.

Axel had pushed me out of my own group, and there was nothing I could do about it. He even started having lunch with them. I still didn't want anything to do with him, so I spent my lunchtime hanging out with Brandon and his crew, listening to him talk about his most recent exploits on DeathLord III: Ultra-Destruction. After a while I stopped hanging around him as well. J.J. and Tangie were keeping to themselves. I hadn't spoken with Tangie since that last weird conversation, and I even missed J.J.'s bossy personality. I found myself staring at the calendar more and more, counting the days to when my third commercial would be shot, which, as it turned out, was scheduled for the last three days of school before winter break.

• • •

I thought it would be great once I was back with the commercial crew; I had the odd sensation that life on the Warner Bros. lot was my real life and that school and all my friends there were sort of drifting away. But every once in a while something would remind me of school and I'd think, *Now they're doing the Secret Santa exchange,* or *Now they're rehearsing for the winter recital,* and I'd feel this weird tugging, like I was Alice in Wonderland, being pulled out of a dream. Then something exciting would happen on the set and I'd forget about that other life, but next thing I knew I'd suddenly feel lonely because there was nobody around who was my age, no one with whom I could just hang out and joke around. I felt like I was being pulled from both sides. And I was beginning to realize my mom was right: You can't have it both ways.

The third commercial had a Western theme, so we were using the Old West town on the Warner Bros. backlot. It started with a card game where a desperado (Edward again) was cheating. He gets into a shoot-out where he and three others destroy the interior of the bar. Finally the toughest-looking cowboy shoves Edward up against the bar, sticks a gun to his chest, and says, "I hate cheaters!" Then I'm supposed to ride in on a horse, jumping through the broken window (my stunt double would do that part), and then trot up to the cowboy and say, "You like bubbles?" I pull a can from my holster, open it, and spray him in the face with the soda. He starts laughing and takes the can. He slaps Edward on the back, and a pile of aces fall out of Edward's coat. They both laugh. Everyone else joins in, breaking out the soda from behind the bar and drinking it like they're all good buddies, even though they're all bruised and bleeding.

We rehearsed my part a few times with the horse, which was a lot of fun. Perry was the horse wrangler, and he was glad to find out that I already knew how to ride, and felt pretty comfortable being on one. He even got the horse to rear up before I said my line, which was scary but fun. Perry said I looked like the Lone Ranger, a character from an old black-and-white TV show that of course I've never seen. I wonder if I can find it on DVD? Once again my part in the whole thing was small, so my rehearsal finished pretty early. Then I just had to wait until they needed me for shooting.

Waiting gave me plenty of time to think about the class holiday party I was missing, which made me feel depressed. I looked for Mo, hoping she would cheer me up. She was wearing a white patent-leather jumpsuit with wide lapels, white boots, and a rhinestone belt. She looked like she'd hopped in a time machine from the seventies. That made me laugh. Since the commercial was about cheating at cards, she taught me how to palm a card. You slide the top card off the deck and hide it in your hand. She also showed me how to force a card, causing someone to pick it from the deck without knowing that you're influencing the choice. That was a lot harder.

For my science assignment, she introduced me to the special effects engineer, who showed me how a lot of the effects in the shoot were done. All the glass that was broken during the scene, from the bottles on the bar to the plate-glass window, was made of a special "breakaway glass," which was really a type of brittle, clear plastic. It shattered like glass but wouldn't cut you if you were hit with it. He said you could make something just like it at home, out of sugar, water, cream of tartar, and corn syrup.

The shooting effects were accomplished by using "squibs," which are little explosive devices, like tiny sticks of dynamite. They're attached to the wall. The actor appears to fire the gun, and then the special effects engineer sets off the squib with a detonator. The squib has wood splinters attached to it, so that when it explodes it looks like the wood has been hit. If the squib is attached to a person, it has blood capsules attached, making it look like the person has been hit. Just as in the second commercial, the whole fight scene was perfectly choreographed down to every last punch. This took a lot of time, so Mo was able to teach me quite a few card tricks.

Perry had brought Jeeves with him again. Jeeves wasn't being his usual mischievous self. He seemed grumpy and refused to put my cap on his head when I offered it to him.

"What's wrong with Jeeves?" I asked Perry when I caught up with him at the craft services table.

"What do you mean?"

"He seems in a bad mood. Haven't you noticed?"

"Maybe he's bored."

"Can I play with him?"

"No, if he's in a bad mood I don't want you messing with him. I don't think I need to remind you. . . ." Perry held up his stump of a finger.

I went back to Jeeves's cage. He really looked sad. "What's wrong, Mr. Jeeves?" I said. "Something got you down?"

It might have been my imagination, but I thought I detected a nod, or at least a change in his expression. "Things aren't so great for me either," I said. "I mean, I'm really grateful for everything that's happened to me. I'm living a life that most people dream of. Every day something exciting happens. But still . . . how did everything get all messed up?!" Jeeves raised his eyebrows. I took that as a show of sympathy.

"Getting into show business was supposed to help me be like everyone else and help me make friends! But I'm more on the outside now than I was when I started! I'm missing everything! And because I lost the friends I had, I'm telling my problems to an orange ape!"

Jeeves just scratched his butt and stared off in the distance. I'm not sure what he meant by that.

I followed his gaze to Perry, who was working with a dusty gray stallion. Something about Jeeves's expression was familiar . . . then I realized I'd seen that same look on Axel, whenever I caught him looking at me. Kind of a hurt look, a little angry, and maybe even depressed. Then I got it. Jeeves was jealous! He was jealous of the horses! And now that I thought of it, Jeeves had looked at Betsy the tiger the same way on the jungle shoot.

I went back over to Perry. "Why do you always bring Jeeves with you?"

"He likes attention. He gets lonely easily."

"Have you been spending any time with him lately?"

"Well, right now I'm busy, Mitch, so no, not today. Don't worry—I'll spend time with him. But let me do my job right now, okay?"

I left him and went back to playing cards with Mo. She was trying to pass it off as a math lesson, but we both knew better. I was beginning to think she wasn't as serious about her job as she had originally claimed.

The next day I decided to fill my free time by making

a video documentary of my day on the set. It gave me a reason to talk to the people who up to this point I'd only been watching from a distance. The main thing I discovered was that people who work in show business come from all over. They are men and women, people of all backgrounds and cultures, people whose families have worked in show business for generations, and people whose parents didn't own a TV set until recently (me). They had amazing stories to tell. Here are just a few:

AMAZING CREW STORIES

1. Lucy, the script supervisor, has a degree in chemistry from Harvard and studied medicine for two years before changing her mind about her career and coming to Hollywood.

2. Arnold, the key grip, is the eighth person in his family to be a grip.

3. Marco, the actor playing the tough card player, waited tables for six years before he got his big break in commercial acting, and now he does stand-up comedy every Friday at the Laugh Factory.

4. Alvin wanted to be a director since he was three years old. He made his first film when he was six. It was about his baby sister turning into a monster.

5. Mo was married twice: once to a fellow little-person actor who died from cancer, and once to an insurance salesman, but that marriage ended in divorce. "It's hard to be in show business and be married to someone outside the business," she said. "It's difficult for your partner to understand and approve of the Hollywood mentality unless they're part of it."

6. Annie, the camerawoman, has written fifty-six screenplays, none of them produced. She has no plans to stop writing them.

7. Jackson, the writer, has a PhD in applied mathematics. He is also an accomplished guitarist and plays in a punk rock band on weekends.

8. Tom, the first assistant director, dropped out of school in eighth grade and bummed around for several years before answering an ad to be an extra in a horror movie. He prefers being behind the camera.

They were all very different, but they did have one thing is common: big dreams. Whether they were brand new to "the business" or had been around for a while, they all dreamed of working on something meaningful, hoping that in some way they'd touch someone with their work.

I put Jeeves in my documentary. When I turned the video camera on him, something incredible happened. He stopped moping around and started hooting and hollering, to the point where I got a little scared.

Perry came running over. "What's going on here?"

"I'm sorry, I just wanted to film him a little. . . ."

"Oh, that's all," Perry said, relaxing. "He's a big ham. Look at him."

Jeeves was making all kinds of faces, peeling back his lips to show off his teeth, clapping his hands, and shaking his head. "Looks to me like he's happy," I said.

"Yeah, he misses being in the spotlight. Last movie he was in was two years ago." Jeeves was now holding on to the bars of his cage and jumping up and down. It made quite a racket. Perry tried to calm him, but he was having too much fun. Finally, Perry turned back to me. "Mitch, you might not want to film him anymore. If he keeps making noise I won't be able to bring him tomorrow."

I nodded and switched off the camera. As soon as I did, Jeeves stuck out his tongue and turned his back on me.

Friday we shot the commercial. It was pretty complicated, so it took all day. After we finished ("wrapped"), we had a little holiday party with cake and eggnog and some hors d'oeuvres provided by craft services. The holiday treats were a welcome change. I was getting a little tired of the craft services food. It wasn't bad, and it was free, but still it was basically the same snacks day after day. I noticed that a lot of the crew, when they were in a hurry, would stand directly over the garbage can with paper plates filled with food. When they were finished gobbling their lunch, they just dropped everything into the can. Mo couldn't stand it. She always insisted we eat at the commissary.

"At what point does the food become garbage?" she said. "When they drop it? When it hits the can? The last scoop that reaches their mouths? It's disgusting. Don't you ever do that. You stay civilized, Mitch."

Winter vacation dragged by. I thought I'd like having a break from school, but since I'd already had a lot of time off from class, I missed it. My mom tried to cheer me up by taking me to a mall to go Christmas shopping, but every five minutes somebody recognized me and bothered me for an autograph or someone would snap a picture of me with his cell phone. My mom was getting fed up with it, and so was I. We decided to buy our presents online instead.

The only halfway fun thing that happened was that Brandon invited me over to a big Winter Wonderland party at his house, but it was very much like the Arabian Nights party. His parents rented an outdoor skating rink and ordered a "snow truck" that created a mountain of snow, kind of like a huge snow-cone machine on wheels. They'd hired a glass blower to make personalized ornaments. Ten different ice sculptures dotted the yard, strolling carolers dressed in Victorian costumes sang throughout the night, and Santa Claus arrived in a sled pulled by eight live reindeer. It was impressive.

But where were Brandon and his crew? You guessed it. Holed up in his room, playing . . . not DeathLord III this time, but the new version, DeathLord IV: Armageddon. It had just come out in time for Christmas.

Skywalker and his family had gone to Cabo San Lucas, in Mexico, for the holidays, which he said they did every year. One day I saw Dash and Axel playing handball in the park on one of the courts with Skywalker's fantasy murals. I really wanted to get a closer look at the mural, but I couldn't bring myself to join them, so I turned around and went home instead.

I did have one guest. J.J. stopped over on Christmas Eve with a big unwrapped box. She looked very nervous. It was the first time I think I'd ever seen her look anything less than completely confident. I thought it was awfully sweet of her to buy me a gift, but according to my mom, if somebody gives you a gift you need to give them a gift too. I tried to remember if there was some book I could give her that I hadn't read yet, or a stuffed animal or something that was lying around in my room that I might be able to pass off as new. I remembered a ceramic duck that still had the price tag on the bottom that my aunt had given me as a souvenir of her trip to Maine. That would do the trick.

"Hi, Mitch," J.J. said, a big smile on her face.

"Hey, come on in," I said. She entered, glancing around. She was wearing a bright blue scrunchie and earrings with blue Egyptian scarabs. She seemed like she wanted to say something but didn't know how to begin, so I tried to help her out.

"Merry Christmas," I said, pointing at the box. Now she just looked confused.

"Huh? Oh. I don't celebrate Christmas, but thanks. Happy Hanukkah." She glanced around again.

"Well, what's the present for?"

She took a deep breath. "Mitch, is your dad here?"

"Yeah, but don't worry, he's out in the yard. He's not going to burst in on us or anything."

"No, no, he's who I came to see. I wanted to show him this."

J.J. placed the box on the table and carefully lifted off the top. On the bottom was a thick layer of Styrofoam, and on the Styrofoam was a large collection of dead beetles, each one pinned to the base with a straight pin.

"This is my bug collection," she explained. "There are a few that I can't identify. I was hoping . . . I mean, do you think he would . . . ?"

"You want him to look at your collection?" She nodded, eyes bright. While I led her to the yard I was still trying to piece together what was going on, but by the time we got there it was obvious. After I introduced her to my dad, he recalled having met her before, at Brandon's party, and J.J. went completely nuts, like he was some kind of rock star, gushing about how much she likes bugs, showing off her scarab jewelry, pointing out all her beetles and telling my dad where she found them.

She didn't have a crush on me! She didn't care about me at all! All this time she had been kissing up to me just so she could get to my dad! I should've seen it earlier; all the clothing and jewelry decorated with bugs, and she was a spider at Halloween. . . . I'd never felt so used, until I realized I wouldn't have a top-notch agent if it wasn't for her and that she really wasn't my type anyway. But still, I felt pretty lousy. While she and my dad gabbed about beetles, I went back into the house.

I spent the next few days sleeping in and watching TV. I took Mo's advice and watched a bunch of old movies (some of them black and white) and practiced card tricks. I taught Bandit to jump from the couch to the coffee table using the reward method of animal training. My mom didn't care for that project.

"Are you bored, Mitch?" she asked after I'd made a pyramid out of forty-five Oreo cookies.

"Yeah."

"Why don't you invite a friend over?"

"I don't have any friends."

"What do you mean? What about Skywalker, or Dash, or that girl J.J.?"

"It's complicated."

My mom sat down at the table with me. "You want to know what I think? I think that you need to reconnect with some of the people you were just getting to know before all this started," she said. We both knew what she meant by "all this." "Have a party. Your episode of *Kick the Bride* is airing soon—you can invite some friends over to watch it."

"I don't think they're interested in being my friends anymore, or watching me on TV," I said. "Dash is jealous and found someone else to hang out with, J.J. and Brandon never really liked me to begin with, Skywalker and Tangie think I'm a snob. . . ."

"Well, are you a snob?"

"No . . ."

"Are you sure?" My mom tilted her head, raising an eyebrow.

"When was the last time you talked to them about something that was interesting to them, and not just about yourself?"

"I . . . well, that's not a fair question. What I'm doing *is* more interesting, Mom!"

"That may be true, but you still need to ask them about what's going on in *their* lives—even if you don't care, it's only good manners. But if they are your friends, you really *should* care. Honestly, Mitch, I think you've gotten a bit carried away with show business. I understand why. It's exciting, new, something you'd never dreamed you'd be doing in a million years. But you *have* changed. At dinner we all used to talk about our days. Now you talk about your day, then you ask to be excused before we're even finished eating."

"Oh. I didn't realize I was doing that."

"I can only imagine you're doing the same thing to your friends at school."

My mom was right. I couldn't remember one thing anyone else had said about him- or herself in a long, long time. I was guilty of really bad manners.

"Did you know Tangie's grandmother died two weeks ago?" my mom continued. "Did you know Dash won a writing contest sponsored by the Daughters of the American Revolution?"

"No I didn't . . ."

"I found out from the class e-mail the head room mother sends around every week. But I'm sure your friends all know."

I felt terrible. So that was why Tangie hadn't smiled in the last few days before winter break. That was why Axel and Skywalker were giving Dash those fist bumps. "I guess I turned into a big creep," I admitted.

"I think there's still a lot of you that can be salvaged," my mom said with a smile. "You know, when you decided to throw yourself into show business, I told you that one of the conditions for my allowing you to do it was that you needed to keep your grades up. You've done that. But you've let something else drop: your sense of balance. You've lost yourself. You need to find yourself again."

Balance. That reminded me of what Tangie had said about her name at the beginning of the school year. She could tell I was totally out of whack; that's why she was avoiding me, not because she was jealous of J.J. What an idiot I was.

My mom went to wash the dishes, and I went to my room to really think about what had happened to me—where I'd started and where I was now. I realized that my relationship with my friends wasn't the only thing that had suffered; a lot of my old interests had fallen by the wayside too. I had twelve things listed on my résumé that I said I enjoyed, and I hadn't done any of them in months.

I looked under my bed and found my guitar case. I tuned the guitar and started playing one of the first songs I'd ever learned, "I've Been Working on the Railroad." My fingers felt clumsy—like thick, dumb sausages—but soon the muscle memory flooded back, and I closed my eyes and played and played. I played everything I'd ever learned, and even though my singing has been compared to the sound of a dying moose, I sang along. I sang pop songs and folk songs and show tunes, and then I made up my own songs.

Once upon a time Skywalker, Dash, and I had talked about putting together a band. Even though Dash had a bad experience with the lyrics, maybe his recent award would give him his confidence back. Maybe it was time to bring the band up again.

PLAN FOR GETTING FRIENDS BACK

1. Apologize to Dash, Skywalker, and Tangie.
   Your head got too fat; you need to address it.
2. Start playing handball again. Find out when Axel is busy after school and do it that day.
3. Ask Dash if you can read his award-winning essay.
4. Ask Skywalker to finally watch "Star Wars Episode III: Revenge of the Sith" (never got around to seeing it!).

5. Suggest putting together a band. Ask Dash to write some of the songs. Find out if Tangie can sing. Even if she can't, she'd be great to have around.

6. Mind your manners, mind your manners, mind your manners!

The first Monday back from vacation, I was all psyched to put my ideas into action. By coincidence it was also the day that my episode of *Kick the Bride* was scheduled to air. I was tempted to send an e-mail to remind everyone to watch, but something kept me from doing it. Turns out that was the best decision I'd made in a long time.

14

Sugar

THE DAY STARTED OUT WELL. IT WAS A bright, crisp January morning, a brand-new year, and I felt excited to turn over a new leaf.

In the school cafeteria I managed to catch Dash alone. I told him I was sorry for getting so full of myself. I was embarrassed by my poor manners, I said. He made some joke, like "What you should be embarrassed about is that haircut," which meant "Thanks, I'm glad we're still friends."

When I told him that over the break I'd been goofing around with my guitar, *he* brought up putting a band together. As luck would have it, over the break he had written a bunch of poems that he wanted to turn into lyrics! Everything was working out better than I had expected.

That night, after I finished my homework, I spent at least two hours playing guitar. My parents had to remind me that my *Kick the Bride* episode was starting. We turned on the television just in time to catch the first joke of the show. In the episode, one of the characters takes a job as a carnival worker. Even my mom, who doesn't care for the show, had to laugh. We were all in a good mood as the show broke for commercials, and I went into the kitchen to grab a snack. I had just opened the refrigerator and was holding my breath so I wouldn't have to smell whatever was stinking it up when my dad called out from the living room.

"Hey, Mitch, you're on TV!"

"But it's too early!" I yelled back. My scene was the second-to-last one in the show; it shouldn't come up for a while, but maybe they'd edited the whole thing differently. I raced back into the living room, eager to see my first appearance on a primetime program. It really was a pretty big deal, no matter how much it had screwed up my social life.

Sure enough, I was on TV, but it was just the Fizzy Whiz jungle commercial.

"Dad, you got me all excited about nothing . . . ," I started to say, but it wasn't the commercial after all—it was a news blurb. "How Fizzy Whiz Soda can harm your kids," a female voice said over the image. There I was, thrusting the can at the camera, saying, "You like bubbles?"

Kick the Bride started up again, but none of us cared about it anymore. We watched the rest of the show in silence. When I finally saw myself come out from behind the carnival booth and say my line, I felt a little sick to my stomach. After the show was over I went to my room. I knew my parents would watch the eleven o'clock newscast, but I didn't want to. I tried to read or play guitar, but I couldn't concentrate. Once I heard the news start up, I reluctantly went back to the living room to watch.

A female voice spoke over the image of Tarzan swinging through the trees. "With childhood obesity reaching alarming levels, the Department of Health and Human Services places blame squarely on the proliferation of junk food in children's diets. They have issued a list of the worst offenders in hopes that consumers will reduce their intake of these severely unhealthy products. Topping the list is Fizzy Whiz Soda, with its extraordinarily high concentration of sugar. It is shown here in a recent commercial, which is clearly aimed at children."

The newscast then cut to a shifty-looking man standing outside a corporate office building. The female announcer's voice continued. "When asked to comment, Fizzy Whiz spokesperson Fred Bergler had only this to say":

"Fizzy Whiz Soda is a popular drink that gives you a nice boost of energy in a variety of unique flavors. Once again, self-proclaimed consumer watchdogs are trying to legislate values. We at Fizzy Whiz believe in the public's right to choose."

Then the newscast cut to two reporters, a man and a woman, sitting at a news desk.

"Very disturbing report, Sheila," said the man.

"Yes, Stan. It's a shame when big business shows so little regard for our youngest, most vulnerable consumers."

"I don't get it, what does it mean?" I asked when it was over.

"They're saying that Fizzy Whiz Soda isn't very good for you," my mom said grimly.

"Well, everyone knows *that*. I mean, who in the world thinks soda is a health food?"

"That's true, but I think they're saying it's the worst of the bunch," my dad said carefully. "This is probably not a good thing."

I went back to my room. I wished on every star that nobody had seen that newscast. It didn't work.

The next morning in school I could almost feel the sideways glances hitting me like spitballs. I could hear the whispers, the snorts, and the snickers. That's the bad thing about being on a popular show like *Kick the Bride*—absolutely everyone had seen it, and everyone knew about the report from the health department. All day Mrs. Samuelson kept giving me sympathetic looks and shaking her head. She probably didn't even know she was doing it, but it was annoying.

"Oooh, bad scene on the newscast last night, dude," Skywalker said at recess.

"What's the big deal?" I snapped. "It's not like I'm forcing people to drink it. Why would anyone blame me?"

"Mitch, you've been in show business now for half a year. Has anything you've experienced made any logical sense? Well, it ain't gonna start now, buddy. Watch your back." Wait a minute. Skywalker was always optimistic about everything, but now even he sounded downright worried. This was worse than I thought, and I already thought it was a disaster!

I found out what Skywalker meant by "watch your back" when I got shoved in the back after going through the cafeteria line.

"Hey, you still pushing that poison?" It was the same big kid who'd given me a wedgie at the beginning of the year. He'd left me alone for so long, I'd forgotten he was even at the school. But here he was, with the same stupid smirk. He seemed to have grown in the past few months.

"I don't know what you're talking about," I lied.

"On the news they said that soda you're selling causes cancer in rats, jerk."

I shrugged. "Oh yeah? Well it's not made for rats," I said.

That response sounded really lame, and as you can imagine, impressed nobody.

"Sure it is. *You* drink it!" the kid said. Everyone laughed. I could tell I wasn't going to win this war of words, so I turned my back on him, forgetting just what a big mistake that was. He made a grab for my underwear, but I dodged him just in time. I dropped my tray, though, and my chicken taquitos rolled onto the ground. It didn't really matter. I'd lost my appetite.

After school my mom took me to the mall to get new sneakers. My old ones had holes in the toes, and the rubber was almost completely peeled off. It was not going to be an exciting trip, but she promised we could get some soft pretzels and smoothies while we were there.

By then I was starving from missing lunch, so we decided to eat first. As we rode the escalator up to the food court on the second floor, I could see the faces of the people on the escalator going in the opposite direction. Was it my imagination, or were they frowning at me? No, it wasn't my imagination. A few of them shook their heads, just as Mrs. Samuelson had done.

We bought two cinnamon pretzels and two smoothies and sat down at one of the tables. "So, I imagine you've had a rough day today," my mother said, but before she could say anything else a woman with five huge shopping bags leaned over our table and butted into our conversation.

"I wouldn't let *my* child drink that Fizzy Whiz garbage," she snipped.

My mom was at a loss for words. I'm sure she was shocked that a grown woman, one who was wearing pearls, for that matter, could have such bad manners. Finally my mom said, "Excuse me, do I know you?" which was a polite way of saying "butt out." The woman didn't take the hint.

"You should be eating healthy food, young man," she said, turning to me. She eyed my sugary pretzel disapprovingly.

"I'm drinking a fruit smoothie. That's healthy," I said meekly. I don't know why, but I wanted points for that.

"Excuse me," my mom said, again. "Don't talk to my son. If you have a problem, you can talk to me. And I'm sorry, but I don't see how our lives are any of your business." My mom stood up.

Don't let the polite "excuse mes" and "I'm sorrys" fool you. My mom was getting ready to rumble. You see, my mom has two sides to her personality: the nervous one that aims to please, and the fed-up one that she calls Mama Grizzly. Mama Grizzly is tough. Mama Grizzly is ferocious. You don't want to wake up Mama Grizzly, but that is exactly what this woman had done.

"I think children should be protected from these kinds of products, not sent out to sell them," the woman continued, unaware of the danger she was facing. "My children only eat organic foods. We don't watch TV either," she added smugly. "To have this young boy out there on the idiot box, hawking that garbage, just to make money . . . it's practically child abuse."

I could tell my mom was doing everything in her power not to grab that woman by the throat and hurl her over the railing. *Don't do it,* I prayed, remembering J.J.'s rules for celebrity. *Please don't cause a scene and get us all arrested and plastered on the front page of the gossip magazines in every grocery store around the country!* I tugged on my mom's sleeve.

"Bad publicity, Mom," I whispered.

My mom hesitated, and then she leaned in toward the woman and growled under her breath, "You are a rude and ignorant busybody. How dare you judge me or my family? Now, if I were you I would walk quickly in the other direction before I do something I regret."

"Are . . . are you threatening me?"

My mom gave her the most sinister smile I'd ever seen her give. It was chilling, like something out of a horror movie. This time the busybody got the point. She bustled away with her bags and her pearls, her nose in the air. I looked at my mom. She was still smiling that sinister smile. I noticed her barely drunk smoothie cup was empty.

"Mom . . . did you . . . ?"

"Oh look at that," she said, innocently turning her cup over. "I must've accidentally spilled my smoothie into her shopping bag. I can be so clumsy sometimes."

We left the mall. Apparently we were going to buy the sneakers online too.

I hoped that the whole thing would blow over quickly, but that news report got a lot of people steamed up over children's health and childhood obesity. People started complaining about the lack of exercise offered in public schools. Reports came out about the rise of fast-food chains in high schools and the unhealthy menus from which students had to choose their lunches. It wasn't just about Fizzy Whiz Soda anymore, but it didn't matter. The brightly colored can and my big dumb face had become the symbol of corporate greed at the expense of children's health.

All week people stood outside the Fizzy Whiz offices, holding up signs that demanded they change the formula of the soda to make it healthy. Even I knew that wasn't going to happen. What did they want, vitamin-enriched, beet-flavored soda? Besides, from what I could find online, the protests weren't affecting the popularity of Fizzy Whiz one bit. It was still making lots of money.

By the end of the week a group of people calling themselves the Children's Health Advocates of Tomorrow (CHAT) had organized picket lines outside any grocery store that carried the soda. We found this out when my mom and I went grocery shopping and ran into these folks before we knew what it was. They recognized me of course and started chanting, "You like bubbles? You got troubles!" over and over again. Someone sprayed us with soda. A store security guard had to step in and escort us to our car. We peeled out of that parking lot like our lives depended on it. Did this mean we would have to buy our groceries online too?

"Never stand out, never stand out, never stand out," I muttered to myself over and over again as we drove home.

"What?"

"I can't believe I forgot my own rule!" I moaned, fighting back tears. "This is what happens when you stand out. You're a target, and you get shot!"

My mom pulled the car over to the curb and shut off the engine. She turned to looked at me. I have to admit, I was losing the fight with the tears.

"No, Mitch," she said. "Don't think that way. That is not what you should take away from all this."

"Everything was fine before I became the center of attention," I said. "Well, maybe it wasn't fine, but I was better off just being a regular loser. Now I'm a loser on a billboard!"

"Now you listen to me. You are going to stand out whether you like it or not, Mitch, because you are a wonderful, talented person, and you can't hide that," my mom said, getting a little emotional herself. "Your father and I always want you to aim high and take chances, and sometimes they won't work out the way you hoped, like this didn't work out, but it doesn't mean you shouldn't try."

"You were right. It was fun and exciting, but it wasn't worth it. I made the wrong choice."

"Mitch, don't you understand? It wasn't the wrong choice! It may not have been exactly what I would've done, but I'm proud of you. I admire your courage. And you love doing it. I could see it in your eyes when you came home from each shoot. You know you love it."

"Yeah, I do. But I don't like missing everything and not having friends around. And I definitely don't like this part!"

My mom stared out the front window for a moment. I could tell she was gathering her thoughts.

"You learned so much, and you're growing so fast . . . I can barely keep up with you. Look. I think you're learning some important lessons here, some pretty tough lessons. But you have to believe me when I say it's going to be all right."

"You have to say that."

"Believe me. I will make sure of it. But please don't ever hold yourself back because you're afraid of attention. You have too much to offer. And I don't want you to quit something just because you hit a snag, not if you still believe in what you're doing."

"But, Mom, I really don't want to do these commercials anymore."

"I know. I know. This has gotten completely out of control. We'll call Mr. Schwartz as soon as we get home and see if he can get you out of it. I'm sure they'll understand that it's just not working out anymore."

"I thought you might be calling," Jeremy said to my mom when he finally returned my mom's call at dinnertime. His voice was as loud as ever, even when he wasn't particularly excited.

"So do you think you can get Mitch out of having to do the other three commercials?"

"No. I don't."

My mom didn't expect that answer. "But . . . I was under

the impression that you were some sort of expert at this kind of thing."

"Helen, I am *the* expert at this kind of thing. I break contracts all the time, but not this one. So what if the product is crap? Mitch is getting face time. And believe it or not this new attention is great for his career. Years from now, people will still remember him. They won't remember why, they'll just recognize that hilarious face. Trust me, Helen, it'll all blow over, and Mitch will be famous."

Mama Grizzly had hairs rising on the back of her neck. "Listen here, Jeremy Schwartz. We trusted that you had Mitch's best interests in mind when you made this deal. Now my son is suffering. He is miserable, and I expect you to do everything in your power to put his life back in order. If that means you have to go crawling back to the Fizzy Whiz lawyers on your hands and knees, begging for forgiveness for your foul mouth and poor manners, just so that they will release him from the contract, then that is what you'll have to do. Do you understand me?"

"Perhaps you think Mitch should have some other repre-sentation." Jeremy's voice had become very cool.

"As a matter of fact I do," my mom answered, the temperature of her voice matching his, icicle for icicle. "But this is something *you* need to fix, because it needs to be done quickly and well. I'm not so ignorant about the ways of Hollywood that I can't see it's all about image. If Mitch is going to have any longevity in this business he has to protect his image. But you have an image too, Jeremy. If you don't get Mitch out of his contract, I will make it my life's mission to smear your reputation and make your life a living hell. People in my family live into their nineties, so my life's mission could last a very, very long time."

Jeremy had to know my mom probably couldn't do that much damage to his reputation—after all, everybody already knew how sleazy he was. My situation was nothing compared with the pile of notorious Jeremy Schwartz stories that circulated around town. Dash had told me a few of them when I'd first signed with Jeremy, before we'd stopped talking. But my mom's speech did make Jeremy realize that he might be dealing with a crazy woman, and judging from my mom's behavior at the mall, he was.

I couldn't hear what he said next, so it must've been something he muttered under his breath. My mom hung up.

"Bravo, Helen!" my dad said. "The last time I saw you give a speech like that, it was to my mother at our wedding, when she insisted on bringing her dog to the reception." He chuckled at the memory, but Mom had a grim look on her face.

"I don't think he can do it," she said. "I don't think he's going to come through."

The next day I tried to keep a low profile. When I got to school I put on my baseball cap, hitched up the collar of my jacket, and headed toward my locker, but I couldn't get anywhere near it. A crowd of kids blocked the hall. They were laughing about something, but I couldn't see what it was. I hung out near the water fountain, waiting for them to leave, but they stayed until the first bell rang.

Once they ran off I could see what the big joke was. Somebody had taped a photo of a really fat man to my locker. He was a morbidly obese person so big he was trapped in his house because he couldn't fit through his door. I ripped it down and went to the main office to get a late slip, but when I got there I just called my mom and asked her to pick me up. I felt like a big baby, but I had already faced a week of fat jokes and other kinds of unwanted attention (example: wedgies). I just couldn't take one more day of it.

As my mom drove me home, we passed the billboard on Sunset Boulevard. Someone had spray-painted a mustache on my face and blacked out a few teeth. Where it once had said, "You like bubbles?" it now read, "You like blubber?"

"Oh for heaven's sake," my mom said, and sighed. "It's

just not fair, Mitch. You didn't ask for this. We'll figure something out."

My mom tried to reach Jeremy on the phone a few more times, but either he wasn't there or he was avoiding her. I spent the day in my room, reading. For lunch my mom brought me a cup of chicken soup, as though I were sick. I *was* sick in a way—sick of show business.

"I finally talked to Jeremy," she said. I could tell from her eyes the news wasn't good. "He said that Fizzy Whiz's boost in sales coincides exactly with this new advertising campaign, and that you are the face of Fizzy Whiz. If we try to break the contract, they will sue us. Apparently there was something in the small print of the contract that protects them from just this kind of situation."

"So . . . what are you saying? I have to keep making commercials?"

"Well, there are only three more left. . . ."

"But I can't go back to school, Mom! It's torture! I hate it there!"

My mom was silent for a moment. "Maybe we can transfer you to another school . . . a private school. We can use the money you're making from the commercial. Of course, since it's a national commercial and a national news story, it would have to be a school where nobody watches television, listens to the radio, uses a computer, or reads the newspaper, like maybe a school deep in the center of the earth, or on one of the moons of Jupiter."

I just looked at her. I had finally done it. I had driven my mother insane. She just gave me a little shrug. "Sorry," she said. "I'm a little upset." She went back to doing whatever she had been doing, and I went back to my room.

At about three thirty the doorbell rang. My mom called up that a friend of mine had brought over the homework for today. I expected that Skywalker would come by to try to make me feel better; he must've seen my locker this morning.

But it wasn't Skywalker. It was Axel.

"Hey," he said.

"Hey."

"I brought your homework over. It's not much, just math and science. I made copies of the chapters out of my books." He held up a big yellow envelope.

"Would you like a snack?" my mom asked. "I'll have fresh cookies in a minute or two." She obviously couldn't tell Axel was my archenemy. Axel seemed to have forgotten this as well. He looked at me hopefully, obviously wanting those cookies, which we could smell baking in the oven.

"Yeah, sure, stay a while," I said, just to be polite. "They're chocolate chocolate chip. Really good."

"Great," he said. I couldn't believe he actually accepted.

After my mom served the cookies and milk, she disappeared into the den to grade papers.

"I knew you weren't sick," Axel said as soon as she was gone.

"Yeah, well, I didn't feel like being teased all day," I said. "That was a great picture you found to put on my locker. Ha ha, very funny."

"I didn't put that there." Axel looked hurt that I would even suggest it.

"So you're not here to gloat about it?"

"Hey, I'm doing you a favor. If you want me to leave, just say so." He stood up.

"No, I'm sorry. Stay. I'm just mad, that's all."

"I don't blame you. I've been there. I know what you're going through." Axel sat back down and grabbed another cookie.

"No, you don't," I said sulkily.

"You don't think so?" Axel put the cookie back on the plate, folding his arms. "Maybe you'd rather be me, a has-been at the age of twelve. I'm recognized too, you know. Everywhere I go, people still call me by the name of my TV character, and then in the same breath they call my show unfunny, stupid, the worst sitcom ever. I don't know if my friends like me because I'm famous or because they really like me." He stared off into space for a moment, and then he shook it off, grabbed the cookie again, and took a big bite.

"Sorry. I didn't know you had it so rough."

"There's obviously a lot you don't know."

"What do you think I should do?"

Axel brushed the cookie crumbs from his shirt. "You've got a great agent. I should know. He dumped me two years ago, after my show was canceled. He can get you out of it. Make him earn his ten percent."

"We tried that. He said he couldn't do it. He said it didn't matter that the product stank, that people would hire me later because they would remember my face, not the product associated with it."

"He's lying."

"How do you know?"

"Because lying is what he does best. Look. Agents do whatever makes them the most money. If you don't get paid for your commercials, then he doesn't make his ten percent, right? He's getting as much money out of you as he can now, because you're not going to last. You're a flash in the pan, the flavor of the month. You will never work as an actor again. You were lucky to get the commercial. Period."

"But Jeremy said . . ."

"Listen, Mitch—and I'm telling you this for your own good—you are a lousy actor. You stink."

Boy, what a jerk! I couldn't believe Axel would say that to me, in my house too! After eating my mom's cookies! But as he sat there with his arms crossed, I realized the smirk was gone, replaced by something else. Honesty. And at that moment it hit me. Axel wasn't being a jerk, he was being a friend.

"I'm really that horrible?"

"Mitch, you're a funny-looking kid. That counts for something in this business, but it gets old fast. Jeremy doesn't want to lose whatever money he gets from this contract because he knows there will never be another one. Okay, fine. Fire him. In fact, you should dump him before he dumps *you*. It's coming, believe me, and at least you should get the satisfaction of dropping the bomb on him rather than the other way around."

I sighed. "Even if I fire Jeremy, that still leaves me having to do the commercials, and there's no agent out there who's going to want to inherit this problem by signing me now."

Axel drummed his fingers on the table, thinking. Then a smile slowly spread across his face. "I've got it." He quickly took a big slurp of milk. "You have to get the Fizzy Whiz people to *want* to release you from your contract."

"And how do I do that?"

"Get them to fire you. Act like a big, spoiled-rotten brat."

"I . . . I can't do that!"

"Sure you can. Child stars do it all the time! And they can get away with it too, because they know they have the power. But you're just on a commercial. There's not as much money riding on you. Yes, I think they would fire you if you caused enough problems for them."

"Well . . . I wouldn't know where to start."

Axel smiled. "I see you writing lists all the time. I'll make a list for you."

AXEL'S SUREFIRE TIPS FOR GETTING FIRED

1. Make unreasonable demands—the more expensive the better.
2. Throw lots of tantrums.
3. Order people around like they're your servants.
4. Refuse to come out of your dressing room.
5. Tell the crew and the director how to do their jobs.
6. Change your lines.
7. Leave a huge mess wherever you go.
8. Ruin the take twenty or thirty times.
9. Arrive late to everything.
10. Spread wild rumors.

"Wow, this is a pretty good list," I said after reading it over. "But this just isn't me. I mean, they'll think I'm playing a game or something. I just can't."

"You sure? Each one of these by itself would make you the least-liked person on the set," Axel said. "Together they're guaranteed to make you public enemy number one. I should know. I've done 'em all. You know, when they canceled *My Mom's a Mutant*, it wasn't because of low ratings, it was because they didn't want to put up with my nonsense anymore."

"Why try to get fired? I thought you liked acting."

"I don't really know. I think I was just bored. I was pretty young when I became famous, you know. I got used to being treated like royalty. Once I got a taste of that . . . that power, all that attention, I just wanted more and more. I guess I wanted to see how far I could go."

"It *is* a great feeling." I sighed. "I'll miss it, I think."

"Yup, you will. I still do. Think of how you feel and multiply it by a hundred. A thousand. That's how I feel." Axel shrugged with a sigh. "Well, you'll just have to get over it and move on." He tapped the list. "It took me four years to ruin my career. If you try to do these all at once, you can get the job done in a day."

"My mom flips out if I forget to say 'please' and 'thank

you.' If she knew I did anything on the list, she . . . I believe she might actually disown me. I'm not kidding."

"All right, just trying to help." Axel stood up and pulled on his jacket. "I'd better go. I've got to get started on that homework. It's just one page of math, but they're all hard word problems, and you have to answer about six essay questions for science."

I stood up and shook his hand, thanking him for bringing the homework over. Then as he turned to leave, I added, "You know, you're not as much of a jerk as I thought you were."

"Yes I am," he said. "I was jealous of you. I still am. I'd do anything to be a star again. All that attention . . . back on the cover of *Entertainment Weekly* . . . man, I'd even do your crummy commercial. I can't help it, showbiz is all I know."

I walked him to the door. He had locked his bike to the railing of the front porch and now started to unlock it. "We should play handball sometime," I said. "I hear you're good."

"You bet I am. I can kick your no-talent butt." He hopped on his bike and rode off.

15

Crash Course

THE NEXT DAY MY MOM LET ME STAY home from school, and the day after that. We talked about my going back on Thursday, but that night we got not one, not two, not three, but *four* crank calls, so we decided I would stay home for the rest of the week.

"This is outrageous!" my dad said after hanging up on the fourth crank caller. "I have half a mind to call the police. This is a form of harassment."

"This is Los Angeles, Grant," my mom said quietly. "The LAPD are busy chasing after murderers, not crank callers."

"I'll talk to the principal, then."

"Don't talk to the principal—it'll only make it worse!" I moaned. Schoolyard rules are very clear.

UNWRITTEN BUT UNDERSTOOD RULES
OF THE SCHOOLYARD

1. Boys don't hit girls.
2. If you hang out where you're not wanted, you're asking for it.
3. If you stand out too much, you're asking for it.
4. If you're a suck-up, you're asking for it.
5. If you snitch, you're asking for it.

I don't think I have to tell you what "it" is. The last thing I wanted was for my dad to snitch to the principal. He'd probably show up to the meeting dressed in that stupid roach costume.

"I can't just sit here and allow this to continue," my dad said.

"Grant, we don't even know who's making the calls," my mom said, irritated.

My dad rubbed his chin. "Well, maybe we should think about moving. . . ."

"We are *not* moving!" my mom said sharply. "This is one problem we won't be able to solve by moving! For God's sake, we've only been in this house for three months!"

"I'm just looking at our options, Helen. . . ."

"That's your answer to everything! As soon as things start to get uncomfortable, we move!"

"'Uncomfortable?' Is that what you call it?" my dad shot back. "I was fired! Blackballed by the entire faculty! That's a little more than just 'uncomfortable,' Helen."

It was time for me to go. I quietly rose from the table and went to my room. I could still hear everything anyway.

"Maybe you should stop getting fired, Grant! That would go a long way toward helping the situation. How many times are we going to uproot ourselves? We're like nomads, wandering in the desert! Moving from one place to another like . . . like cockroaches!"

There was a long pause. "I'm sorry. I guess . . . I'm just unpopular with my colleagues."

"That's the understatement of the year."

"What do you want from me, Helen? Do you want for me to give up the cockroaches? Is that what you want? Fine, I'll give up the cockroaches."

Yes! I thought to myself. *Give up the cockroaches! For once we can live normal lives!* But my mom's affection for my dad got in the way once again.

"No, don't give up the cockroaches, Grant," she said, her voice softening. "That's not what I want. You would be miserable, and that . . . that would just break my heart. We should all be so lucky, to find something in this world that we love so much." There was a pause, and I can imagine her putting her hand on my dad's shoulder, and my dad patting it with a grim but grateful smile.

"But you could try to tone it down a bit, couldn't you, dear? Grant . . . this obsession . . . people just can't take it! You're a brilliant scientist! *You* know it, *I* know it, *they* know it! They just don't understand your—your passion."

"You don't seem to have a problem with it. . . ." There was a pause.

"I'm different. I guess that's what makes us good together." Pause. "It's not the cockroaches, Grant, it's the constant moving, the running away, the 'fresh starts.' There are only so many fresh starts a person can take. I'd rather just face the music and be an outcast."

"Perhaps that's how you feel, Helen, but would Mitch? He's the target this time, not us."

Again there was a long pause. I stopped holding my breath. It seemed like maybe the worst of it was over, so I left my room, just as my dad was coming up the stairs.

"Oh, Mitch!" He sounded surprised, and maybe a little embarrassed. "I suppose you heard all of that."

"Yes."

"Well, don't worry. We'll figure something out. It's a tough nut to crack, but we'll get through it."

"Dad, can I ask you something? In private."

"Sure, of course." My dad followed me back into my room. We both sat on my bed. "You know, Mitch, I have to say I admire how you've held up under all this. You've got guts, son. I wish I had your guts."

"Dad . . . I overheard you guys talking about why we move all the time."

"Oh." My dad ran his fingers through his hair a few times, and then turned his gaze to the ceiling with a heavy sigh. "The moving. That's been my fault. My 'crazy enthusiasm' for cockroaches seems to turn people off."

"Except J.J.," I reminded him. "She likes it. Of course, she's a little nuts herself."

That got my dad to smile. "Yeah, she's . . . interesting, all right." He looked back at me. "Let me tell you something, Mitch. Everyone has baggage. Do you know what I mean? 'Baggage'? It's parts of your personality, your personal history, your quirks and passions. You carry this baggage with you wherever you go, and people either accept it or they don't. Well, my baggage is filled with cockroaches. They travel quite well, you know . . ." Dad was about to veer off topic, so I interrupted.

"Dad, what is it that you like about cockroaches anyway?"

He blinked at me. "I've never told you?"

"No, but I've always wondered. Everybody else in the world thinks they're really gross."

My dad's eyes brightened. He got this big smile on his face and shifted around on the bed, like he was settling in for a long time.

"Well, I didn't always like cockroaches, you know. When I was about your age, I hated them. Our apartment in New York was infested with the things. We couldn't get rid of them. My mother, your grandmother, was at her wit's end. She thought having cockroaches was a sign of filthy living habits. She was ashamed, so I was ashamed. We tried traps, fumigation, stomping on them. . . . At first my goal was to kill each and every one, but after a while, I realized we were fighting a losing battle. Sure, we could get them to scatter for a day or two, but they always came back. Then something strange started to happen. I started to admire them. I started to root for them. Roaches are survivors, Mitch. They are here to stay. The oldest fossil from a cockroachlike insect dates to three hundred and fifteen million years ago. That means the cockroach has seen the dinosaurs come and go!"

"I guess that is pretty cool," I said. I meant it.

"I know! It's incredibly cool!" my dad blurted. "So what's their secret? They adapt. They can eat almost anything, they can live in extreme environments. . . . These are some hardy little suckers! Their bodies adjust so quickly that as soon as you find one pesticide that kills them, they become resistant to it. Some people think they would survive a nuclear holocaust. And that's just some of what they can do. They're amazing creatures, and you can be sure they will outlive humans."

"Wow. I never thought of it that way," I said. "An animal that just lasts forever." That thought started to sink in. And then it occurred to me that people don't hate roaches because they're disgusting. . . . After all, they're just a type of beetle. No, people don't like roaches because *they can't get rid of them.* They're survivors. They're winners.

My dad left my room after giving me more vague assurances that things would turn out okay. After he was gone I thought about what he had said about roaches, about surviving. Adapting. Maybe that's what I needed to do. Running away will keep you alive, but like the hardy roach, if you want to win you have to come back. You have to adapt. You have to learn. I wasn't going to solve anything by trying to avoid my problems; I couldn't run away from them or hide from them, even if I wanted to. I needed to adapt, come back, and fight.

Look out, Hollywood: Roach Boy was back.

• • •

I was waiting on the porch for Axel when he rode up on his bike to deliver my homework the next day. "I thought about your list," I said. "I'd like to give it a shot, but I can't pull it off by myself. I want you to be my acting coach."

Axel blinked. "Really? Me?"

"Yeah. You know I'm a crummy actor, but maybe you can teach me. I'll pay you. . . ."

"Forget about it, Mitch. Friends don't pay friends. Besides, it should be easy. Any kid knows how to be a brat. It's second nature."

"I don't think I can make anyone believe that I've become a complete jerk overnight," I said. "I could really use your help."

"Sure thing. When do you want to start?"

"I shoot the next commercial on Monday, so we'd better start right now."

"Fine." Axel smiled. "Don't worry. In just a few days I'll have turned you into the rottenest kid on TV."

Axel was good. He had taken acting classes since he was five and could transform himself into characters right before your eyes. He could cry in an instant, speak in twelve different accents, and mime just about anything. He talked to me about how you have to forget yourself and become whatever it is you're trying to play, and as I watched, he transformed himself into a crippled beggar, a gluttonous Frenchman, a sleepy security guard, a frantic mother, a hundred-year-old weight lifter, and a crying preschooler—with real tears!—all in the span of five minutes.

I applauded when he finished.

"Thanks, but this isn't a one-man show, Mitch." Axel laughed after giving an exaggerated bow. "I'm trying to show you how to throw yourself completely into a character. You can't be self-conscious. You can't be afraid to look foolish."

"But that's one of my biggest fears—looking like an idiot."

"Not anymore. Now you're an actor. Looking like an idiot comes with the job. Think about it. Actors have to be willing to do almost anything—kiss people they don't like, perform naked, get hit with food, play morons, jerks, and all kinds of disgusting people. . . ." He grinned. "Actually, that's the *fun* of it!"

"That's just what Edward said—you know, the goofy guy in the commercials with me."

"A wise man, Edward. Okay, let's loosen up." Axel started swinging his arms from side to side.

"Exercises?" I said. "We don't have time for that."

"You need to have stamina to be an actor, Mitch, and you need to have control over your body. Let's start with stretching your face muscles." He opened his eyes and mouth as wide as he could, then scrunched them up tightly, then twisted his lips from one side to the other, and finally he stuck his tongue out several times.

I copied his face exercises. Then I stretched my arms, legs, neck, and back. My muscles really did feel looser, and I felt ready to work.

"Let's try some mime," Axel suggested.

"I'm not performing at the mall for spare change, am I?"

"Mime is a great exercise to train your body." Axel thought for a moment. "Okay, pretend you're drinking a glass of water. First, picture the glass: how big it is, how heavy it is, what's in it. . . . Is it something you like or something you don't like?"

"What difference does it make? It's invisible."

"It makes a difference! It adds believability to your performance! I want to be able to guess what you were drinking after you're finished."

I thought about some incredibly sour lemonade I'd made the day before, and the little juice glass I drank it out of, and then tried to imagine it on a table. I reached out my hand.

"Don't let the glass change sizes as you bring it to your mouth. And when you put it down, I want to be able to tell where the table is."

I "drank" my sour lemonade about ten times. I must have improved a tiny bit because Axel was able to guess what I was drinking on the fourth try. Still, I wasn't very good at it. My "table" kept changing heights, and the "glass" looked more like a sandwich. It didn't matter, though; I just had fun doing it. It felt great to be hanging out with someone my own age.

"Okay, okay, let's move on to something else," Axel said, realizing we were getting nowhere with mime. "You need to try some method acting."

"What the heck is that?"

"Well, it's kind of hard to explain, but it's when you use your own memory to help you give a realistic performance. For instance, when I cried half an hour ago, I did it by remembering how I felt when my dad died."

"Oh. I didn't know. I'm sorry."

"It's okay," Axel said. "It was a while ago. But I remember it like it was yesterday. So I can cry pretty easily. What you have to do is latch onto an emotion from somewhere inside yourself—a strong memory of something—then you put yourself there in the memory and say the lines you've been given. Except you don't have lines, you're just going to make them up yourself as you go along. You know, improvise."

"Make them up? You mean, on the spot? How am I supposed to do that?"

Axel crossed his arms. "Look, haven't you ever pretended you were sick so you could get out of taking a test?"

"Uh . . . maybe."

"Well, how did you do it? You remembered what it felt like to be sick, and then you concentrated on it, you put yourself in that memory, and then your body sank into it, your voice changed, your eyes changed. . . . That's all it is. The hard part isn't doing it, it's keeping it going. Because if you drop it suddenly, people figure out you were just pretending."

"Okay, okay. I get it. So where do I start?"

"Let's start with what you know."

Axel told me to say the line "Thanks for inviting me to your birthday party" first as though I had the stomach flu, then as if I hadn't slept all night, and then as if I was really offended. I did the same thing with the line "I'll have the hot dog, not the cheeseburger," and once again with the line "May the Force be with you."

After I'd done the exercise to Axel's satisfaction, we started goofing around, saying different phrases with the wrong emotions.

"I just won the lottery—I'm a multimillionaire," I moaned.

"I have only two weeks to live," Axel squealed, as though it was the most thrilling news he'd ever heard.

"What a cute little puppy," I snarled.

"I've got to go home, we've got tons of homework today," Axel said with a sigh.

"No, no, you should've said that in a happy voice . . . like, 'Yippee! We've got tons of homework today!'"

"I said it sadly because we really *do* have tons of homework today," Axel said, gathering up his backpack. "And you have more than I do, since I finished the reading assignment in class." I walked him to the front door and opened it for him.

"You know, you did pretty well for your first time," he said, turning. "I can't come tomorrow, but I'll see you on Sunday."

For the first time, I was sorry to see Axel go.

At the end of the weekend Axel came back, but this time he brought Dash and Skywalker with him. My mom and dad were out, so I served the guys big slices of the pumpkin cake my mom had made the night before.

"Wow! What's that awful smell?" Skywalker howled when I got the milk out of the fridge.

"I don't smell anything," I lied, quickly shutting the door. "Let's start. What are we doing first?"

"Improvisation," Axel said, pouring himself some milk. "Improvisation is basically just making stuff up and going along with whatever is tossed your way. So here's the scene:

You are an obnoxious, spoiled, pampered child star. Let's say Skywalker is . . . your tutor."

"Skywalker is about three times as tall as my tutor."

"We're pretending, Mitch."

"Okay, okay. What do I do?"

"Just be really obnoxious and rude. Demand something totally outrageous."

I thought for a minute, but my mind was blank. "I really don't know where to start."

"How badly do you want to get out of this?" Axel said, crossing his arms.

I thought again. "You're looking very ugly today, Mo," I said in my snobbiest voice. "I insist you get me a muffin."

The guys just stared at me.

"Wow, that stunk-ola," Skywalker finally said. "That's the best you can do . . . I mean, the worst you can do?"

"Look, we don't have much time," Dash said. "Improvisation is too advanced for him, Axel. What Mitch needs is a script." He pulled some folded paper from his back pocket and handed it to me. "After Axel called me last night, I went ahead and wrote something up for you. It's not a real script, it's just a list of some lines you might say to different people on the set."

I started reading.

TO THE DIRECTOR

1. How about some more close-ups? (Point to your face.) This here is the money shot, dummy.
2. What do YOU know? Call me when you win an Oscar.
3. You're nothing but a hack.

TO THE WRITER

1. I'm sick of saying the same thing over and over. From now on I'm going to say, "Here's a squirt in your eye!"
2. How come they have more lines than I do? I'm the star! Give me more lines!
3. This isn't funny—it's just stupid.

TO THE PROP MASTER

1. This heavy soda can is hurting my wrist. Make one for me out of Styrofoam.
2. Is this really what you wanted to do with your life, or are you just another failed screenwriter?
3. Whoops, I bent the can. Get me a new one. (Repeat ten times.)

TO THE CRAFT SERVICES GUY

1. This food is crap!
2. Where are my lobsters? I'm on an all-shellfish diet!
3. Yecch! What did you put in here, dog food?

TO THE FIRST ASSISTANT DIRECTOR

1. I know where to stand—get your paws off me!
    (Then stand in wrong place.)
2. Your breath stinks. Did something crawl down your
    throat and die?
3. (Shout from dressing room) I'm not coming out
    until the first AD leaves the set! He keeps giving
    me the evil eye!

And that was just the first page. "I can't say any of these things!" I blurted. "These are horrible!"

"They're *supposed* to be horrible!" Dash said. "Practice them over and over until they become second nature. If you combine these lines with Axel's list of suggestions, you can't lose!"

For the next two hours we practiced. I memorized the lines; they weren't that hard to remember. Axel taught me how to sneer, how to look really bored, and how to pretend to ignore someone. It was everything he did to me the first day we met. I pointed that out to him, and he laughed.

"Oh yeah, I guess I was doing that," he said. "Sorry, I was trying to act like a jerk."

"So that was just an act?"

"I think so."

"Or are you just acting now? You know, acting like you're a nice guy?"

Axel shrugged. "It's always an act, Mitch. It's always an act."

That sounded a lot like what Tangie had said, about how we're always playing a role. Suddenly I felt a little sad. I missed Tangie. I'd really messed up with her, big-time.

"So . . . you think you're ready for tomorrow?" Axel asked, misreading my expression as worry.

I put on my lousiest sneer. "What's it to you, butt head?" I shot back.

"By Jove, I think he's got it!" Dash exclaimed in a British accent.

"Not so fast." Skywalker removed a box from his backpack. "Now it's my turn." He opened the box. Inside was an electric razor. A chill ran down my back.

"That isn't for what I think it's for . . . is it?"

"Directors can't stand it when an actor drastically changes his appearance," Skywalker said, rubbing his hands together with an evil grin. "The Fizzy Whiz Company picked you because you look wholesome, all-American, and slightly goofy.

Well, there's nothing we can do about the goofy, but we can definitely make you less wholesome." Then Skywalker lowered his voice, impersonating Darth Vader, and said, "Come, Luke, join the dark side."

One hour later I had a purple Mohawk. Somewhere in the middle of the haircut, I wondered how I would keep this from my mom, but I immediately realized it was impossible. I'd have to tell her everything. She wouldn't like it, but I didn't think she would blame me. After all, she'd gone off the deep end herself.

After making fun of my new haircut for twenty minutes, Axel and Dash had to go home. Skywalker was the last to leave. It took us a while to clean all the hair off the bathroom floor and to wipe up the dye that had spilled in the sink. Finally he gathered his stuff together, taking one last satisfied look at his creation (my head) before heading out.

"Break a leg," Skywalker said. Then his eyes lit up. "I have a great idea! What if you . . ."

"I'm not going to break my leg!" I snapped.

"Just a thought," he said with a small shrug, and he took off down the block.

When my mom and dad came home from work and saw my new look, they were both very, very upset. I waited for the yelling to end and then calmly explained to them what

I was doing. I showed them the "script." I talked about my conversation with my dad about adapting, surviving, and not running away from problems.

Then something unexpected happened. My mom burst into three minutes of nonstop laughter, ending with another couple of minutes of snorting and hiccupping. "Well, you're not running away, that's for sure." She giggled in between hiccups. She didn't seem to mind that my "script" required that I become rude, selfish, and downright mean. I guess if you want something badly enough, manners go right out the window.

"Give it a shot, son," my dad said, a little surprised at my mom's outburst. He put a firm hand on my shoulder. "I think you make a darn good roach."

From my dad, that's the greatest compliment in the world.

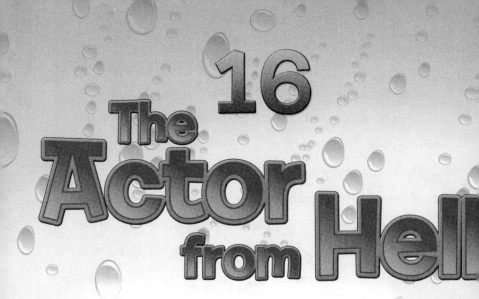

16

The Actor from Hell

MONDAY MORNING MY MOM GIGGLED and hiccupped all the way to Warner Bros. Studios. She wanted to stay to see what would happen, but she knew she wouldn't be able to keep from laughing, so she just dropped me off. But not until we finished a leisurely breakfast at a nearby restaurant, just to make sure that I was an hour and a half late.

I have to admit, I was nervous. I'm not perfect, but I'm generally not irresponsible, and I've never intentionally done a mean thing in my life. When I was a little kid, my mom and dad did a pretty good job hammering into my head that you should always treat people the way you would want to be treated. "How would that make *you* feel?" is a worn-out phrase in our household.

WORN-OUT PHRASES IN
THE MATHIS HOUSEHOLD

1. How would that make YOU feel?

2. Give it a shot.

3. Mind your manners.

4. Did I give you permission to do that?

5. Of course I trust you, but . . . (then an explanation why not in this instance)

6. The dog did it.

7. The dog did NOT do it.

8. Somebody, and I'm not saying who, needs to . . . (instead of just saying "Mitch needs to")

9. It's complicated.

10. When I was your age, I had to . . . (do some horrible chore)

The only way to get through it was to keep reminding myself I was just acting. Besides, I was starting to think it was about time someone considered how *I* felt! I was being attacked from all sides for something that wasn't my fault. I wasn't willing to take the hit for Fizzy Whiz. I had to get out of it. I just had to.

Tom, the first assistant director, was the first person to

notice me. He charged up to me, yelling, "Where have you been?" I removed my baseball cap, and his face dropped.

"Good Lord Almighty, Mitch! What the heck did you do to your hair?!"

I sneered at him. "What does it *look* like I did?" I bumped into him as I brushed past, and right away I felt horrible.

I went to the classroom trailer and found Mo reading a horse-racing magazine. When she saw me, her eyes widened. "I don't know what you're trying to pull, kid, but it ain't funny."

"Well, neither are you," I retorted. It didn't make much sense, but she got the point.

"I'm too old for this." She pulled out her deck of cards and dealt a hand of solitaire. "Do what you want, class is dismissed."

I went to the craft services table and picked through the food, making a mess. Tom brought over Alvin, who looked ready to kill me.

"What the hell do you think you're doing, Mitch? Is this some kind of game?"

"Do you mind? I'm eating here," I snapped. "And how come there aren't any crabs or lobsters? I'm on an all-shellfish diet!"

Perry walked over with a parrot on his shoulder that he was wrangling for the pirate-themed commercial. "Hey, what's buggin' you, Mitch?"

"Your face," I answered tartly.

"Get me his agent on the phone," Alvin growled to Tom. "The kid must be on some kind of weird medication. And get him his friggin' hat."

"*You're* on some kind of weird medication, judging from your directing, you overpaid hack," I said. I thought I was going to faint. I stumbled to my dressing room, unlocked the door, and slammed it behind me. I shouted, "I'm not coming out until Brandy leaves the set! She's giving me the evil eye!" My stomach lurched. I threw up that great breakfast I'd just eaten with my mom, right into the trash can. I guess I wasn't such a great roach after all. Do roaches throw up when they get nervous? I don't think so.

"Making yourself sick, huh?"

I whirled around. Mo was sitting quietly on a chair behind the door. "How'd you get in here?"

She shrugged. "Magic."

"Well, get out, you're not welcome in here. . . ." I started to cry. I couldn't help myself. What a disaster. She came over to me, stood on a stool, and put her hand on my shoulder, shaking her head and clucking her sympathy.

In between sobs I told her everything I'd been going through: how I had stopped going to school, how strangers were yelling stuff at my mom and me, how my billboard had been destroyed with graffiti.

"Hey, fame is a double-edged sword, kiddo. You're the king of the world one day and on the dung heap the next. The public is fickle and sometimes downright nasty."

"But what can I do?"

"Well, your agent should be able to do something. . . . Who did you say it was?"

"Jeremy Schwartz." Mo shook her head and hopped down from the seat.

"Forget it. He won't do anything. Having a shark for an agent is also a double-edged sword. He'll make a lot of money for you, but he'll stop taking your phone calls when you're in trouble."

"So you think he was lying when he said I was too valuable to the Fizzy Whiz Company and they would never let me out of my contract?"

"No, he was probably telling the truth there," Mo said. "I've seen this sort of thing happen before. They'll sue you for breach of contract. It can get messy, and it's probably not worth it. I'm sure your parents don't want a prolonged lawsuit sucking up all their money. So you can stop trying to make an enemy of everyone on the set. The crew doesn't have a choice, you know—they're stuck with you. They work very hard, and it's not fair to make them suffer."

"But what can I do?"

"You're a nice kid, Mitch. Everyone says so. Don't ruin your reputation. Just put your head down, keep a low profile, and get the job done."

"There must be another answer," I moaned.

"Not unless you can think of a way for the Fizzy Whiz Company to make more money without you," Mo said. "I wish I could do some real magic—you know, wave a wand and send you back in time so that you'd let someone else get the part, but unfortunately all I know are a few tricks." She pulled a coin out of my ear and smiled. "C'mon," she said. "Let's go to work."

I didn't have a chance to explain anything to Alvin. He was boiling mad about all the time wasted and just wanted to get started. It had already gotten around the set that I had a new attitude problem, so the crew kept their distance from me. I guess that's what I deserved. My little stunt that morning had only made things worse. The only people who approached me at all were the hairdresser, who found a wig for me to wear, and the costumer, who gave me the Fizzy Whiz cap, which couldn't hide the fact that the wig didn't look quite right.

The set was dressed for the pirate theme. The builders had constructed the ship on rockers so that when they moved back and forth it would match the motion of a boat at sea. The whole thing had been erected in front of a green screen. After the commercial was finished, the special effects coordinator would replace the screen in postproduction with a background of the ocean.

We ran through the scene a few times. During a sword fight between the pirate (Edward) and the swashbuckler, the Fizzy Whiz Kid was supposed to climb up the rigging, say "You like bubbles?" to the pirate, and then spray him with the soda, but of course it wouldn't be me climbing those ropes, it would be my stunt man. In reality I would say my line on a completely different mast that had been built closer to the ground in another part of the soundstage.

Because of all the time I'd wasted, when we broke for lunch we still hadn't shot anything. The actors and crew all left for the commissary. I chose to stay behind. I was still too ashamed to hang out with them.

Someone else had stayed behind too. Jeeves stared at me through the bars of his cage, looking as miserable as ever.

"I know how you feel, Jeeves," I said. "It's a rough business."

Jeeves answered by removing my cap and putting it on his head. He looked a little happier. He peeled back his lips, showing off his teeth, and then blew a loud raspberry. I laughed, even though I was still pretty upset.

"Maybe if I were a real actor, I'd be able to take it," I said to the orangutan. "But I'm not a real actor. I couldn't even play a realistic brat. Axel was right all along. I'm nothing but a goofy face. A monkey could do what I do."

Jeeves nodded, chomping his teeth together and clapping his hands. I stared at him. Slowly an idea began to form in my head. I tried to shake it off . . . it was too crazy. But the more I tried to get rid of it, the stronger it grew. It was perfect. *He* was perfect! But it could never work. And yet . . .

"Oh, what the heck," I said out loud. I grabbed two nearby cans of Fizzy Whiz Soda and handed one to Jeeves. Naturally he started to shake it. I shook mine too. Then I popped open my can, and the soda spurted out. Jeeves squealed with excitement. I got another soda and did it again. Still nothing, but he screeched happily as the soda gushed out. The third time I did it, Jeeves put his finger on the tab of his soda, and I immediately gave him a treat. The next time he opened his up, spraying all over his cage, sending him into more gleeful squeals and hooting. I gave him another treat.

In no time we had gone through twenty sodas and had made an incredibly sticky lake of Fizzy Whiz on the floor. Jeeves not only knew how to open the can but also to wait until I gave him the signal before he did it. I already knew Perry's signal to make him blow a raspberry, so we practiced that a few times too, for good measure.

After I mopped up the soda, I took a deep breath. "Okay Jeeves," I said. "I'm trusting you. Please, please, please do not bite my finger off."

I opened his cage. The next instant, Jeeves was up in the ship's rigging. I realized that the entire time we had been rehearsing, he had been watching the stuntman climbing up and down the ropes, and he had been sitting in his cage getting jealous! Of course he would! He was an *ape*, after all!

For the next forty minutes, I taught Jeeves to wait until my signal, then climb up the ropes and open the can, and then stick out his tongue and blow a raspberry. As soon as I saw people drifting back to the stage, I grabbed his hand and led him to my dressing room, praying that Perry wouldn't notice he was missing from his cage.

Soon I heard Tom's familiar knock. "You're up, Mitch," he said.

"Er, I'm not feeling well. My stomach is bothering me again," I called out.

"Mitch, you're not pulling another fast one . . ."

"No, really," I said. "Just run through it once without me. Please . . . I'm just drinking some ginger ale. I'll be right out."

After Tom left I opened my door so I could hear when they started the rehearsal. I dressed Jeeves in my coat and cap. The coat dragged on the floor. I removed the bottom row of empty soda cans from the elastic loops and rolled up the sleeves.

"Well, that'll have to do. Don't trip," I said to the eager ape. I heard Edward and the other actor clash swords on the set. I checked outside the door of my dressing room to make sure no one was around, and then carefully made my way with Jeeves behind the green screen. The soda cans in the coat clinked together as he scrambled after me, but fortunately the noise from the sword fight covered the sound.

Then I heard my cue. I stepped out onto the stage with Jeeves and gave him a hand signal. In an instant he had scrambled up the rigging and was running toward the two very surprised sword fighters.

Jeeves didn't even wait for the signal—he knew exactly what to do and when to do it. He opened the can, squirting Edward right in the face. Then he shrieked and did a flip, clapped his hands, and blew a wet raspberry, handing Edward the soda can. Edward, stunned, took a drink, which sent Jeeves into a series of flips. Then the orangutan waggled his butt, doing what looked like an "in your face" dance. Jeeves was improvising!

Everyone on the stage had broken into screaming laughter from the moment Jeeves had run up the rigging, and each additional face he made caused a fresh eruption of howls. Alvin grabbed Perry.

"My God, Perry! You are brilliant! If they could hand out Oscars for practical jokes, I'd give you one right now. How long did it take you to put this together?" Alvin spotted me as I moved forward from the shadows. "Mitch, that temper tantrum this morning . . . that was all part of this, right? That was just a setup, to throw us off?"

Perry looked at me and scratched his head. "Alvin, I had nothing to do with it."

"Come on, you're kidding, right?"

"I swear on a stack of Bibles and my mother's grave . . . that is, if she were dead."

"Well, then who . . . ? How . . . ?" Alvin turned to me. He could tell from my face that I was responsible, but he asked anyway. "You did this, Mitch? By yourself?"

I hesitated, then nodded. Alvin shook his head and gave a low whistle.

"I don't believe it! One thing I have to say, you've got guts, kid. Excellent joke!"

"It's not a joke," I blurted suddenly. "I'm just desperate!" Then everything came pouring out of my mouth like it was a broken faucet; I couldn't stop. I told them everything—about how I couldn't go to school, about the lady in the mall, the grocery store protest, the billboard, my failed appeal to Jeremy, and about Axel's plan. A small crowd had gathered as I went on, and I felt more and more embarrassed. I was admitting that I couldn't take the heat and that I didn't care about the "show going on." I just cared about myself.

At first there was only silence. Then I started hearing murmuring from the crew.

"Poor kid."

"Hey, I've been there."

"I miss having a normal life too."

"This business is hard on the little guys. Do we have to ruin the kid's life?"

"Why is it that the nice people are always destroyed by this industry?"

The grip came over and put his hand on my shoulder. "Hey, I feel for you, Mitch. Anyone makes fun of you, just know I got your back."

"Me too," said the set designer.

"Who cares what other people think?" said Lucy, the script supervisor. "Didn't anyone ever tell you not to read your reviews? What do they know?"

Mo tugged on my sleeve. "Think of it as baptism by fire. What doesn't kill you makes you stronger."

Edward placed a hand on my shoulder. "You're one of us, Mitch. Outsiders just don't get it. They don't know what it's like to have this pressure, to be so vulnerable to public opinion. But all of us here, cast and crew, we're you're family. We're here for you."

The crew gathered around me, patting me on the back and giving me more encouraging remarks. I realized then what kept people in this strange and brutal business. It wasn't just the desire to be in the spotlight, or needing a place to show off their "artistic expression." It wasn't just to have a fun, cool, awesome, glamorous job, and it wasn't just the money, though all those things were part of it. It was the people, this amazing community of creators, living in a world of dreams and imagination, helping each other reach for the stars.

Suddenly I felt a lot better. Maybe it would all blow over. But even if it didn't, I wasn't alone.

Then a voice rang out from the back of the crowd.

"I like the monkey." Everyone turned to see Mr. Baxter, the executive from the Fizzy Whiz Company.

"I guess I'm supposed to be the bad guy here, so I'll play my part. It's true, Mitch, I did get a call from your agent, and I wasn't going to let you out of your contract. It's bad business to dump a successful advertising campaign. But frankly, the monkey is funnier. If you want out, I'll let you out . . . now that you've found a suitable replacement for yourself."

Everyone cheered. Jeeves held his hands together, shaking them over his head like a champion.

"Let's call it a wrap for today," Alvin said. "We've got to rethink the script now that there's been a casting change."

"Let's have a good-bye party for Mitch!" the craft services guy suggested. "Everyone meet back on the stage in an hour— I'll have it all set up."

"Oh, please don't," I said. "Don't go to any trouble for me. I've caused enough problems."

"No trouble at all. I already have chips and guacamole and a whole bunch of cupcakes. I don't want them to go to waste."

"Besides, people in show business will use any excuse to have a party," Mo added. "Wedding shower, baby shower, welcome party, good-bye party, holidays, finalize your divorce, buy a new car, show off your new purple Mohawk . . . anything goes."

An hour later we were all laughing, eating cupcakes, and toasting one another with plastic champagne flutes filled with sparkling cider. People started telling Hollywood horror stories: about projects that seemed like winners but suddenly went right into the toilet, about projects doomed to failure from the beginning, about working with mean executives and out-of-control actors. Each story seemed funnier than the last, and I realized that in a few years my story would sound exactly the same.

"I can't lie," I said to Mo as the party wound down. "I am

going to miss this. It was all so exciting . . . but maybe too exciting."

"Mitch, I didn't want to tell you this when I met you, but I knew from the beginning you wouldn't last."

"Thanks a lot!"

"It's not a criticism, it's just the truth. I've seen all kinds of people come and go in this business. The people who last are the ones who not only have the talent for the job they've chosen but also the personality. You didn't have either. You see, an actor needs to be self-centered to survive. It doesn't mean he's selfish, or that he doesn't care about other people, but it's his job to focus inward. That self-centeredness also gives him a nice tough shell that protects him from a fickle public. You simply aren't self-centered enough, and you can't act worth a lick. Sorry."

"I know, I know. I've been told." I scanned the group of people all chatting and enjoying themselves: the costumer, the set decorator, the grips, the first AD, the cameramen. Each one an important part of the dream factory.

"Well, where would you place me?" I said, taking a sip of sparkling cider. "What job matches my personality?"

Mo straightened her glasses and studied the crowd as well. "Hmm, I'm not sure I know you well enough. You tell me. Do you have a good ear? You could be a sound technician. Do you have a sense of style? Then set dressing or costumes might be up your alley. Are you a visual person? Do you think in pictures? Then maybe you could be a cameraman, or better yet, the director of photography. That's where you find the true visual artists. But craftspeople are all detail oriented. Perfectionists."

"That's not me," I admitted.

"Do you like to write? The writer is a storyteller, the creator and architect of the project. They've got to have a good ear for dialogue, be able to create unique characters, explore themes, and use words to convey everything in their head to the director."

"No, you lost me with 'Do you like to write?'" I said.

"Well, the director is also a visionary. He or she has to take the script and bring it to life. He also has to be a good leader and communicator, but most of all he has to be organized. He has to know what he wants: what shot, what look, what take, what actor, and so on. So directors make lists, lists, and more lists. . . ."

My ears perked up. "That's me! I make lists! I love lists! I'm very organized!"

"And you're a great communicator," Perry said, joining us. "You're especially good at communicating with animals. Before you make up your mind, I can tell you something else you have a real talent for: animal training."

My eyes widened. "You really think so?"

"I sure do. You knew that Jeeves was unhappy, and you knew why he was unhappy. You seem to be able to read animals without any formal training at all. That's a gift. Not everyone can do it. And even experts make mistakes." He waggled his finger stump. I wished he would stop doing that.

"And as smart as Jeeves is, you still got him to learn something new. You taught him to open a soda can in less than an hour. That's pretty darned good."

"I just did what you did," I said. "I rewarded him with snacks."

"Well, I'm impressed. If you aren't completely sick of show business, you can hang out with me at the ranch and I'll show you the real nuts and bolts of what I do. Not only do I train animals, I train trainers. You could sit in on those classes."

"I don't have to think about it—I'd love it," I said. "I just need to get permission from my parents. . . ."

"Have them call me." Perry handed me his business card. It had a picture of Jeeves dressed as a director, shouting through a megaphone.

"Hey, spring break is coming up in March," I said. "Maybe . . ."

"March would be a great time to visit," Perry said, laughing. "We'll be getting ready for a film that's being shot in August about a dog that robs banks. Should be fun. You can join me on the movie set. You've seen how commercials work, and now it's time to move up to the big leagues."

"Whoa, are you sure you wouldn't rather spend that time with your friends?" Mo cautioned. "I mean, isn't that what you wanted? To get back to leading a normal life?"

"I can't help it." I grinned. "I've got the show business bug."

"Well then," Mo said with her wry smile. "Here's to new adventures in the dream factory."

We clinked our plastic glasses.

Hooray for Hollywood!

The Last List

WHAT HAPPENED NEXT

1. My mom and I fired Jeremy Schwartz. He screamed at us over the phone, but J.J. told me later that he had expected it and that he wished me well.

2. Brandon stopped inviting me over to watch him play video games.

3. Skywalker, Dash, Axel, and I held handball tournaments every weekend. We were evenly matched.

4. I hung out at Perry's Animal Kingdom ranch during my entire spring break. One of his rabbits bit my finger, but it was not bitten off.

5. I finally did go to a JPL open house for the public and saw all the cool things Tangie had described. She made sure I went; she's the one who took me there.

6. My mom can't drink a fruit smoothie without laughing (and hiccupping).

7. We found out what that bad smell in the fridge was: some really, really, really old cabbage soup.

8. Jeeves became a phenomenal hit as the Fizzy Whiz Chimp, even though he is technically not a chimp. They made twelve commercials with him altogether. He makes all sorts of public appearances and was even on "The Tonight Show." He loves the attention. I am not jealous, not one little bit.

9. My father was hired as a consultant for a science-fiction movie about killer cockroaches. He was in hog heaven. Skywalker's dad was hired to do the makeup, and he created a six-foot-tall cockroach for my dad. We keep it in our doorway as our homemade burglar alarm.

10. Skywalker, Dash, and I never started that band. Instead, we decided to make a movie starring Axel. It was a comedy about a kid who desperately wants to fit in at a new school and who goes through all kinds of crazy stunts to try to make friends. Dash wrote the script, J.J. was the producer overseeing the project, and Skywalker designed the sets, costumes, and visual effects with Tangie. I was the director. . . .

"Cut!" I said, turning off my digital camera. "Dash, you're not on your mark."

"Hey, I'm a writer, not a performer. . . ." he protested, searching the ground for the masking-tape X.

"Yeah, well, in this movie we're all doing double duty. Everybody's a performer or we won't have enough people for the scene you wrote. Let's take it from the top. . . ."

"Mitch, I think everybody needs a break," J.J. said from her producer's chair. She owned one herself and had brought it from her house. She took her producer role very seriously.

"Okay, okay," I agreed. "Everybody take ten." I walked over to Axel and Tangie, who were eating snacks from our makeshift craft services table—basically a cooler stocked with some iced tea and lemonade (no soda—anything but soda), a bag of pretzels, and a lemon-blueberry pound cake my mom had provided. "How do you think it's going?" I asked.

"Really good. It's a fantastic script," Tangie said.

"Yeah, it's perfect. I just have a few lines I'd like to change," Axel joked, knowing Dash was within earshot.

"Over my dead body," Dash snarled, also kidding.

"Yeah, about this script," I said, turning to Dash. "This wouldn't by any chance be based on somebody we know, would it?"

"It is a complete fabrication," Dash said innocently. "I

don't know where I get my ideas. They just crash into my head, like a thunderbolt."

A car pulled into our driveway and a woman stepped out. It was Mrs. Mulligan.

"Axel, it's time to go! I've got to get you to that audition by six o'clock!"

"Okay, okay," he said, waving to her. "I'll see you Saturday, Mitch."

"Shooting starts at ten a.m. sharp!" I reminded him. He shot me a thumbs-up as he headed toward his mom's car. "Hi, Mrs. Mulligan!" I shouted, waving.

"Hello, Mitch!" she shouted back. We both knew better than to get within thirty feet of each other. It was safer that way.

Dash, J.J., and Skywalker also had to go home, but Tangie stayed behind to help me clean up. It was the first time I'd had alone with her since . . . everything. We had never really talked about it, for which I was very thankful. She probably knew from her parents that when you get bad publicity you just put it behind you and, as Dash would say, accept it and move on. Still, there were things unanswered, things about which I was curious.

"So, Tangie," I started casually as we put the leftover food back in the fridge, which was now wonderfully cabbage-stink-free. "You hate acting and everything about it, don't you?"

She hesitated. "Yes."

"I knew it! Why?"

"I've seen what craziness my parents have had to put up with. How they're judged by their appearance, not their ability, and how cruel movie critics can be. I've seen how hard they have to work to keep some sense of balance in their lives, and to make sure our family is normal . . . well, as normal as it can be. Fortunately they're successful without being really famous." She rolled her eyes. "Fame. Everyone who's never had it wants it, but I wouldn't wish fame on my worst enemy."

"Well, then why the heck didn't you warn me?" I sputtered.

"Number one: I didn't think you'd be 'discovered.' Usually those cattle calls are just a waste of time. Number two: You wouldn't have believed me. And number three: I gave you my best advice. I think you're finally following it."

Ah yes, that crazy advice she gave me when I was in line at the recreation center. "Don't act; just be." Now it made sense.

Once everything had been put away, Tangie picked up her jacket, ready to go. I stopped her, putting my hand on her arm.

"You know, you never told me what role you play," I said.

"What do you mean?" She tilted her head, her eyes big and so blue. They were the color of blue popsicles, which is about as blue as it gets.

"Well, a while ago we had a conversation where you were talking about the roles different people play in life, and you mentioned everybody but yourself. You said Skywalker was an artistic rebel, Dash was an intellectual, I was a fathead. . . ."

"Oh, yes, I remember," she said. "I'm glad you switched roles. Now I'd say you're . . ." She narrowed her eyes as though looking deep inside me and then smiled. "You're the hero on the verge."

"Hey, I like the sound of that! On the verge of what?"

"Well, that remains to be seen, doesn't it?" She smirked and zipped up her jacket. "It's getting late. I'd better go." She started heading outside.

"Not so fast," I said, stopping her again. "What about you? What are you playing . . . the space case?"

She just smiled and gave a small shrug.

"No, that's what you want people to think," I reasoned, "but you're deeper than that. There's a whole lot going on in that blonde head of yours. . . . Let me see, I'm going to go with . . . philosopher? Visionary? Angel?"

Suddenly her eyes were clear and striking, the dreamy quality all but gone. "Getting warmer," she said with a grin. And with that she was out the door, heading down the front path. I hesitated but then followed, catching up with her at the sidewalk.

She turned to me with a smile. "Going my way?"

"Definitely."

We turned down the street, walking into the sunset.

THE END.

CREDITS ROLL.

Acknowledgments

THE ENTERTAINMENT INDUSTRY IS LIKE
no other. It is art and commerce put together in an often
uncomfortable fit. It's a difficult business but an extraordinary
one: exciting, aggravating, fun, vicious, glamorous, frustrat-
ing, gratifying, and heartbreaking. Believe it or not, I love it
all. This book is a love story.

I remember what it was like when I first arrived in
Hollywood, fresh out of college, looking for work as a writer.
I felt like Alice in Wonderland; everything seemed so bizarre.
The people, the parties, the work—it was funny and wonderful
and weird and grotesque all at the same time. I knew one day
I'd have to put my experiences in a book. This is that book. My
goal was to convey what Hollywood is like through the eyes of
a newcomer, so that people who are not in the entertainment

industry can get some idea of what it's really like to work and live here, the good and the bad.

My research for this book was done over the twenty-five years that I've been working as a television writer. I've been on many shows, and my natural curiosity has always led me to talk to people on the set. Over the years I've asked hundreds of people what their job is like, how they got it, what their favorite projects were, and if they have other aspirations. The list is so long I couldn't possibly include everyone's name, but I'd like to thank everyone with whom I've worked—writers, actors, crews, executives, and agents—for the wealth of material they have provided me, even though they probably didn't know it at the time.

I'd also like to thank a few people by name who have been my mentors and taught me more about writing for this business than anyone: Jim Kearney, the late Kim Weiskopf, David Lloyd, Bob Ellison, Rick Kellard, Gary Miller, and Chris Cluess.

Thanks also to my husband, Patric M. Verrone, who was there when my first magazine article was published for the *Harvard Lampoon*, which indirectly set the course that my career would follow, and who has supported my writing ever since. I also thank him for his work as board member and president of the Writers Guild of America, an organization that has improved the lives of all writers in the entertainment industry. As always I'd like to thank my book agent, Laura Williams, and my editor, Maggie Lehrman, for their support and suggestions.

Last but not least I thank my three children, Patric, Marianne, and Teddy, for whom I write all my books, and who inspire me every day of their lives.

About the Author

MAIYA WILLIAMS was born in Corvallis, Oregon, and grew up in New Haven, Connecticut, and Berkeley, California. She attended Harvard University, where she was an editor and vice president of the *Harvard Lampoon*. She is a writer and a producer of television shows and lives with her husband and their three children, a Labrador retriever, and a variety of fish in Pacific Palisades, California.

This book was art directed and designed by Chad W. Beckerman. The text is set in 12-point Adobe Garamond, a typeface originally drawn by the sixteenth-century French engraver and punch cutter Claude Garamond. Garamond modeled his typefaces on those created by Venetian printers at the end of the fifteenth century. The modern version used in this book was designed by Robert Slimbach, who studied Garamond's historic typefaces at the Plantin-Moretus Museum in Antwerp, Belgium. The display font is Shag Lounge. The illustrations are by Michael Kolesch.